After checking the way was clear, Zoya crawled to the gap and wedged herself in. If she was ever going to escape, it had to be now. She tugged the straps of her parachute one last time, then leaned over the edge of the airship. For a short way, the hull ran straight down, then it curved inwards and away. Beyond, was sky. Way down, a mile or so below, she made out the faint orange smudge of a city at night. It looked beautiful and warm against the black. Guess that's what I'll aim for.

Zoya closed her eyes and stepped off the airship. A silent scream escaped her mouth. It continued for a few seconds before Zoya realized that free-falling from an airship wasn't half as bad as she'd thought. Indeed, it was peaceful. There was no wind whipping past her cheeks, no roaring sound as she cut through the atmosphere. Just peace and quiet.

Zoya opened her eyes.

Something was wrong. The ghostly night-time clouds floated along in exactly the same formations as before, and the hull was still at her back. She looked to her left, then her right. Nothing. It was only when she looked above her that Zoya saw what had to be the biggest man on the planet. His arm, bigger than Zoya's waist, was clamped around the straps of her parachute.

For Dominika

OXFORD
UNIVERSITY PRESS

Great Clarendon Street, Oxford OX2 6DP

Oxford University Press is a department of the University of Oxford.
It furthers the University's objective of excellence in research, scholarship,
and education by publishing worldwide. Oxford is a registered trade mark of
Oxford University Press in the UK and in certain other countries

British Library Cataloguing in Publication Data
Data available
ISBN: 978-0-19-274701-3
1 3 5 7 9 10 8 6 4 2
Printed in Great Britain
Paper used in the production of this book is a natural,
recyclable product made from wood grown in sustainable forests.
The manufacturing process conforms to the environmental
regulations of the country of origin.

Five reasons you'll love this book . . .

...through the clouds on the sky-thief ship, *The Dragonfly!*

...roducing Zoya Delarose, a heroine worth fighting for!

Could you make it through a meteor storm?

...rush up your sword-fighting before you meet ...endon Kane, the best villain since Darth Vader!

A gripping cat-and-mouse chase across the skies!

PREPARE FOR A
Swashbuckling Adventure!

Zoya burst out from behind the barrels and sprinted towards the parachutes. As she moved, she determined which was the least wrecked, leapt into the air and tugged at it. At first the bag caught on the beam, but with a few yanks Zoya was able to loosen it. She stood, arms raised beneath the falling chute, praying she'd catch it before it thudded to the deck. The bag landed in her arms before she could even finish the thought, and she spun on her heels and pumped her legs, slinging the pack on her back and bolting back to her hiding place.

There, she adjusted the parachute so it sat comfortably on her shoulders, then tightened the straps. She took the canopy cord in her hand and gave it a pull. It seemed OK. Zoya poked her head above the barrels and scoured the passage for somewhere to jump. Halfway along was a break in the wood. It was small, but it would have to do.

DAN WALKER

OXFORD
UNIVERSITY PRESS

1

The first thing to appear in the office ceiling was a foot.

This emerged from between the roof struts, and was followed by a leg and then the body of a young girl. All three swivelled and kicked as if dancing. After a second, the movement ceased. The foot, the leg, and the backside hung in the air, then Zoya DeLarose descended to the floor. She landed in a crouch, her eyes glinting in the darkness.

Clear, she thought.

Zoya crossed the floor and flicked a switch, bathing the room in orange light. No sooner had her eyes adjusted than she jumped at her squinting reflection in the mirror. Her blonde, bobbed hair was a shock of spikes and cobwebs, and her face scratched. Her clothes were ripped and torn.

'Damn,' she muttered, pulling at a loose thread. 'I like this top.'

She was standing in the office of her orphanage owner and headmaster, Mr Whycherley. The room had changed little since Zoya's last visit. Mr Whycherley was a plain man and his office reflected this, with the usual cabinets, calendar, coat-stand, kettle, mugs, and waste-paper bin. His only quirk was an obsession with sky thieves and their airships, a fascination Zoya shared. Despite repeated warnings for the children to stay away from the pirates ('ruffians and scoundrels, never done a day's work in their life!'), their rogue nature had done little to deter Mr Whycherley from amassing the world's biggest collection of sky thief memorabilia, including paintings, keyrings, and airship models. Even the office's bookcase contained a section dedicated to thieves. Zoya spotted one of these books now—*Sky Thieves: Stealing the Sky*—and made a mental note to ask Mr Whycherley if she could borrow it the next time they had one of their 'chats'.

Only one other object in the room stood out: Mr Whycherley's ornate wooden desk. Zoya knew her locket was inside. Mr Whycherley had confiscated the pendant three days before as punishment for organizing a competition to see which of her friends could eat the most eggs without throwing up. The answer had been none, of course, and Mr Whycherley had demanded her locket for a week. To Zoya, this was torture. Every hour that passed without her locket gnawed at her insides, until she could barely breathe. The locket was her everything, her good-luck charm, the only thing she truly owned in the entire orphanage. It had only been a matter of time before she made a rescue attempt.

Zoya reached into her back pocket and pulled out a hairpin. She'd learned many tricks growing up in an orphanage, but none more useful than lock-picking. She reshaped the pin until it resembled a paperclip, then slid it into the lock on the desk's top drawer. Tilting her head to help her concentrate, she started to manoeuvre the pin left and right, jiggling it in the lock, before she heard a click.

Zoya opened the drawer. Inside, her locket glowed in the lantern light. She placed her hand on the pendant, breathed a sigh of relief and glanced at the open ceiling.

'Right, better get out of here.'

'Too late, I'm afraid,' said a voice from behind her.

Zoya wheeled around, but she already knew who it was. Only one person in the orphanage had a voice that deep. 'Hello, Mr Whycherley.'

2

'Zoya DeLarose, I might have guessed,' said Mr Whycherley.

'I wasn't expecting you for another five minutes,' said Zoya.

'Ah, apologies,' said Mr Whycherley. 'I've never been good with time. Now, would you mind telling me what you're doing in my office and why there's a roof tile on my desk?'

Zoya took a moment to think.

'For me to believe it,' continued Mr Whycherley, 'it's going to have to be an incredibly good excuse, Zoya, even for you.'

Zoya thought of every excuse she could: that she'd seen a fire, that she'd heard a burglar, that she'd had a nightmare. None rang true. Mr Whycherley was more likely to believe she'd sleepwalked there than any nonsense about fires and burglars.

'Sir,' said Zoya, 'I can't think of anything that wouldn't get me into more trouble.'

'Wise,' said Mr Whycherley. 'How about you tell the truth then? That would make a change.'

Mr Whycherley stared at Zoya as she twisted her foot into the carpet, and realized he'd never get the truth. He removed his jacket and slung it over the coat hook. He was a tall man with an unkempt forest of chestnut hair, giving him the perpetual look of someone who'd just escaped a hurricane. His shirt was always creased, stained, and two sizes too big. Overall, he resembled more a disorganized pirate than an orphanage owner.

In spite of this, Mr Whycherley was a force to be reckoned with. He'd inspired generations of down-on-their-luck orphans to make something of themselves, a fact that had earned him a special place in Zoya's heart. Indeed, he was the only person she'd ever truly respected.

Mr Whycherley knew this and used it to his advantage whenever necessary. Now was such a time. He sat behind his desk with his feet up on the table and stared at the floor for a long time without speaking. He let the silence fill the room. Eventually, Zoya looked away. When she did, Mr Whycherley spoke. 'How long have you been at my orphanage, Zoya?'

'Twelve years, sir.'

'And how many times have you been in my office during that time?'

'I don't know, sir.'

'No? Well, luckily I keep a record.' Mr Whycherley opened the top drawer of his desk and took out a red book.

5

He placed this on the desk, opened it near the centre, traced a line down its page until he found Zoya's name, then snapped it shut. 'Eighty-eight,' he said, 'eighty-nine if you count this one. That's eighty-nine times I've had to address your behaviour. I'm starting to think my words are going in one ear and out the other without staying the night.'

Mr Whycherley arched his eyebrows in anticipation of a response, but none came. 'Do you want to know something?' he asked.

'Sir?'

'I've been doing this job a long time. I've seen hundreds of kids come through my doors—some crazy, some nasty, some plain dumb. I've even had bright kids, although those are rare. I'll tell you something, Zoya: you are, without a doubt, the brightest kid I've ever had under my care.'

Zoya smiled.

'That's not a compliment,' said Mr Whycherley. 'See, it's easy to be smart. It's something you're born with. What's difficult is deciding what to do with your brains. I don't think you're doing anything with yours.

'Now, I've told you everything you need to know to stop yourself winding up here,' he continued. 'I've told you to get your head down, read some books, get some grades. You want to fly, don't you?'

Zoya winced. Mr Whycherley was right. She'd long dreamed of escaping the orphanage and vanishing into the sky. Whether this was as one of the post office's freighter pilots, as a soldier in the Aviation Army, or even as a crew member on one of the notorious sky thief airships, Zoya couldn't care less. All that mattered was getting into the clouds.

'Well, you could. You could be a pilot, a lawyer, or a doctor, anything. But it's up to you, Zoya. I can't do it for you.'

Mr Whycherley paused to draw breath. Zoya watched the cogs of his brain turn. After a moment, he leaned down and reached into the drawer Zoya had unlocked earlier. From inside, he brought Zoya's locket — an oval, inky pendant swinging on its chain. Zoya reached out to grab the locket, but Mr Whycherley lifted it out of her reach. 'I presume this is what you were after?'

Zoya glanced at the locket, then at Mr Whycherley. She nodded.

Mr Whycherley shook his head, then tossed the locket to Zoya. 'Confiscating that did no good, did it?'

Zoya clasped the locket around her neck. For the first time in days, the gnawing in her stomach disappeared.

'Part of me doesn't think it's worth punishing you,' said Mr Whycherley. 'It won't stop you next time. But that wouldn't be fair on the others.' He ground his teeth, then scanned a calendar above the bookcase. 'Ah, that'll do.' He turned back to Zoya with a mischievous grin. 'There's a trip to the aviation museum in the morning.'

7

Zoya's heart leapt. A trip to see the world's greatest collection of sky ships!

'Mr Maxim's taking the younger kids. You're going to go with them. My treat.' Mr Whycherley winked.

Zoya's heart sank at the mention of the toddlers. 'But . . .'

The man fixed Zoya with a stare. 'You're going,' he continued, 'and depending on reports of your behaviour, we'll decide whether there needs to be any further punishment. Understand?'

Zoya opened her mouth to speak, then closed it and nodded. Mr Whycherley swung his feet off his desk, stood up and opened his office door. 'Now get out of here before I change my mind.'

3

Garibald Amstad's Fabulous World of Flying Machines had been founded by the world's richest airship manufacturer ('If you can fly it, we can build it!'). Amstad wanted to give something back to all the people who'd bought his cheap airships and made him a multi-millionaire.

Once the rabble of toddlers had been shepherded through the doors, they were greeted by a procession of freighters, airbuses, tourist transports, battleships, cruisers, and sky thief airships.

'Ladies and gentlemen, and little ladies and gentlemen, welcome to the Fabulous World of Flying Machines!' said the tour guide assigned to their group for the day. 'If you'd like to drop your belongings behind the counter, I'll get ready to take you on your fabulous flying tour.'

The guide was a pear-shaped man. He wore a green suit and bowler hat, and nestled atop his upper lip was a slug moustache that fanned out at the sides.

'My name is Rodger Bartholomew Panklehurst and

I'm going to be your guide for the day. My employer, Mr Amstad, has told me how special he thinks you all are and he's asked me to give you an extra-special tour. You, young man,' he jabbed a finger at one of the younger kids in Zoya's group, 'what's your name?'

The child froze, his finger still up his nose where he'd been picking it.

'M-M-Marvy . . .'

'M-M-Marvy, I like it. Marvy, how do you think most people get around the Fabulous World of Flying Machines?'

Marvy glanced at his teacher Mr Maxim, who nodded his permission to answer.

'Walking?'

'Precisely. Walking. Do you think the children of Mr Whycherley's Orphanage should have to scuff up their boots?'

'Yes,' said Marvy, trying to please.

'Absolutely not!' said Rodger Panklehurst. 'Let fine guests like you walk around all day? Not a chance! For our extra-special guests, we reserve something extra-special.'

On the wall behind the guide was a red button with a 'do not press' sign tacked beneath it. Rodger strode up to the button, glanced back at the children with a conspiratorial wink and pressed it. There was a small *click*, then the wall behind him slid away, revealing a railway and a line of carriages in the shape of Amstad's famous airship. The younger children gasped, and even Zoya had to take a breath. After a moment of awe, the kids leapt on board and jostled for the best spots, as Mr Maxim clambered into the last available space. Rodger leapt onto the platform at the front and spread his arms. 'Who wants to see some flying ships?'

The children cheered.

'Who wants to see the first airship ever built?'

'Yes!' shouted the kids.

'Who wants to see the remains of the *Spangled Dangler*, the first airship flown around the world by the magnificent Wangle brothers?'

'We do!'

'Who wants to see,' said Rodger, savouring the words, 'Gruesome Captain Grimybeard's black ship of doom?'

'We do!'

'In which case,' said Rodger, 'buckle up, because we've got to FLY!'

For Zoya, the Fabulous World of Flying Machines was a revelation. To see the airships she'd read about, solid and shining—it nearly blew out her brains. So many playtimes had she spent pretending to be the Wangle brothers with her friends, or making them walk the plank as Gruesome Captain Grimybeard, that being amongst the real things was like walking into a storybook.

Zoya returned to the craft that had most fascinated her: Grimybeard's ship—a black behemoth with turbo-boosted engines and an artillery section that would have given the Aviation Army's a run for its money. Zoya ran her hand along the ship's keel, its iron cold to the touch. Down the way, an arch opened into the hull. Milling about outside were a group of visitors who dipped their heads and stepped inside. Zoya followed. She emerged into a huge, lamplit cabin, where families had stopped to eat at rows of benches. The entire wall beyond was given over to paintings of sky thieves, working up in a pyramid from least daunting to most menacing. Zoya recognized a few of the thieves—Fixyx, Goldshatter, and the man in whose ship they were resting, Grimybeard. The only thief without an image was the man at the top, a pirate so merciless that few had met him and survived: Lendon Kane.

Zoya selected a bench in front of the wall and pulled out her lunch. Soon after, a harried Mr Maxim flopped down beside her. 'I give in,' he huffed. 'If Mr Whycherley wants the kids to see this place so much, he can bring them himself!'

Zoya chuckled as Mr Maxim broke off to reprimand a nearby orphan for throwing a sandwich onto the deck of Grimybeard's ship.

'I still can't believe Mr Whycherley likes airships,' said Zoya.

'Loves them,' said Mr Maxim.

'How did he get into them?'

'The Aviation Army. He nearly joined when he was younger. He was about a week from basic training when he dropped out.'

'Why?'

'The orphanage. A friend of his offered him their factory after losing a game of cards and Mr Whycherley thought it was too good to turn down. He lived on the streets himself when he was a kid. I think that's what gave him the idea of giving you lot a home. He turned the factory into an orphanage. I'm sure he planned to get back to the army at some point, but the orphanage just sort of took over.'

'What about you?' asked Zoya. 'How did you end up there?'

'That's easy: Mr Whycherley. Before starting at the orphanage I had a job offer elsewhere. Same work, better pay.'

'Why didn't you take it?'

'Because when I had my interview with Mr Whycherley, I knew I was talking with a great man. And my dad said to me when I was little, "find a great man and learn from him". So I did.' Mr Maxim bit into his sandwich and stared up at the wall of thieves. 'You kids don't know how lucky you really are.'

Zoya thought of all the second chances Mr Whycherley had given her. She knew what Mr Maxim meant.

4

The traffic on the way back from the museum was even worse than usual. Zoya sat on her own at the front of the transporter, away from the rest of the kids. Ordinarily, she'd have grown annoyed at the hold-up, but that afternoon she didn't mind. She wanted time to think. She took her locket from beneath her shirt and clutched it in her hand. Closing her eyes, she focused on her thoughts. After a minute, she managed to disappear into the quiet of her mind.

Mr Whycherley hadn't been exaggerating when he'd told Zoya it was the eighty-ninth time she'd been to his office. Indeed, those were only the times she'd been caught. Had she been reprimanded every time she'd done something wrong, the number would have been closer to three hundred.

Zoya wasn't proud of her behaviour. And she wasn't proud of letting Mr Whycherley down. He was the only adult she'd ever met who demanded she respect herself. 'If you don't respect yourselves, children,' he was fond of saying, 'don't complain when no one else does.'

Back on the transporter, Zoya opened her eyes. It was time for a change. From her back pocket, she grabbed a pencil and some paper.

> *Dear Mr Whycherley,*
> *I'm sorry for letting you down. It won't happen again.*
> *I'm not going to spend my life climbing in roofs.*
> *Zoya.*

In the corner she doodled a smiley face, then she took the paper, folded it as small as she could and slipped it in her pocket.

Eventually, the transporter rounded the last corner before the orphanage and the reason for the hold-up became clear. Blocking their path was a crowd that spilled off the pavement and onto the road. So big was the mob that it formed an immoveable wall. Every head in the crowd faced the orphanage, straining to see above those in front. Zoya followed the line of their gaze and glimpsed another, larger crowd outside the building. Mr Maxim saw the same thing and turned to the driver. 'Stop here please.'

The driver pulled over.

'What's going on?' asked Zoya.

'I'll find out,' said Mr Maxim. 'Stay with the little ones.'

Mr Maxim jumped down from the bus, jogged across the road and started to cut through the crowd, heading directly for the orphanage. Something felt wrong. Zoya shouted at the driver to watch the kids, then swung herself onto the cobbled streets. She sprinted after Mr Maxim, weaving between clumps of people. Closer to the building, she spotted a cordon that had been hidden from the transporter. It hung a yard above the ground and ran in red and white.

'Doesn't look good,' she heard someone say.

Lined up on the front lawn were her fellow orphans. Their teachers—pale-faced, huddled together—chatted quietly. The last thing Zoya wanted was to get caught before she'd worked out what was happening, so she kept one person between her and the teachers and sneaked down the main path towards the front door. From there, she had a decent view of the scene for the first time. The entire orphanage was wrapped in the red and white cordon. Posted at intervals along this were pairs of Aviation Army soldiers, identifiable by their broad shoulders and impeccable burgundy uniforms. Zoya pondered briefly whether she could sneak past them to get inside, but judged it too risky and returned her attention to the crowd. If only she could find someone she knew, someone she trusted.

5

The crowd around Zoya was dense, some people straining to see what was going on inside the building and new arrivals wandering in from nearby streets. It was while scanning these for a friendly face that Zoya first noticed the man in black.

He stood apart from the rest of the crowd, wearing a charcoal suit and black overcoat. On his head he wore a top hat, out of which sprouted thick, greasy tufts of hair. He was a tall, slim man whose body was out of proportion—his torso longer than his legs—giving him a peculiar, unstable look. A bushy moustache clung to his upper lip.

Zoya caught herself staring, and it was a moment before she realized the man was staring back. His pale eyes burrowed into Zoya's, and he smiled—not a warm smile, but one so cold it froze her to the bone. She gazed a moment longer, unable to look away, before a large lady stepped between them. When the lady had passed, Zoya looked back to where the man had been, but he was gone. Before she could gather

her thoughts, she heard a shout. 'DeLarose, I thought I told you to stay on the bus!'

Mr Maxim marched across the lawn towards her.

'What's going on?' asked Zoya.

'I don't know.' Mr Maxim nodded at a pair of soldiers over his shoulder. 'Those idiots don't believe I work here.'

'Is it something bad?' asked Zoya.

'I'm sure everything's fine. Now get back to the bus while I sort this out.'

Mr Maxim marched off again towards the Aviation Army soldiers. Something about the panic in his voice made Zoya even more determined to stay. She followed him through the crowd and stopped a few feet away, behind another group of people. From her hiding place, she had a clear view of Mr Maxim and the soldiers—big, wide men with fierce brows. They appeared to be apologizing. 'Sir, we're sorry. We were under orders not to let anyone through unless they had identification. We've been told who you are now. You can pass.'

The soldiers stepped aside.

'I don't want to get through!' snapped Mr Maxim. 'I've got a transporter full of hungry children over there who want to get back into that building. Now, do you want to tell me what's happening or do I need to speak to your commander?'

The soldier who'd spoken before glanced at his colleague, who nodded for him to continue. Zoya crept closer.

'Mr Maxim, there's been an incident. A break-in. Two men entered after lunch. They were looking for a child. From what we can gather, Mr Whycherley confronted them . . .'

The officer trailed off. He pointed over his shoulder at the orphanage. A man and a woman emerged from the side door wheeling a trolley, upon which lay something large covered in a blanket. It took Mr Maxim a moment to realize what he was seeing. Not Zoya, though. Zoya felt it straight away, like a knife slicing through her heart.

Mr Whycherley was gone.

6

All of Zoya's breath left her. She felt her world collapse, everything floating away—the soldiers, people, trees, buildings, transporters, everything. Voices in the crowd seemed to reach her from miles away, like she was at the bottom of an ocean. Zoya hadn't known a world without Mr Whycherley. He'd been the only stable thing in her life since she was less than a year old. If Mr Whycherley was gone—if that really was it—then something in the world had broken. Zoya could feel that as sure as she could feel the tears on her cheeks.

It took a moment longer for the news to hit Mr Maxim. A minute passed before he was able to pull himself together. He took a handkerchief from his pocket, wiped his eyes and took a breath. 'What about the kids?' he asked. 'Were any of them hurt?'

'The kids are fine,' said the soldier who'd spoken before. 'Another teacher took a whack on the nose and Mr Whycherley . . .' The soldier paused. '. . . well, the kids are fine.'

'And you mentioned they were after one of the children. Do we know who?'

'Yes,' said the officer, fumbling in his pocket for his notebook. 'I've got it right here.' He thumbed the pages until he found the one he was looking for. 'Her name was, let me see . . . Zoya DeLarose.'

Zoya's blood rushed to her cheeks. Her first instinct was to run, to get away from the orphanage and everything that had happened. But she knew nothing about the intruders, or what they looked like. Without this information, she'd be in as much danger running as she would be staying. She held back.

'DeLarose,' said Mr Maxim. 'What do they want with her?'

'No idea,' said the soldier, 'but I know my commander wants a word with her as soon as possible.'

'Zoya's been with me all afternoon,' said Mr Maxim. 'If you want her, she's in that transporter—'

Before he could finish, Zoya stepped forward. 'I'm here.'

Mr Maxim whirled around to locate the voice. His face whitened when he saw Zoya. He marched up and walked her back to the soldiers. The officers exchanged a glance. 'This is DeLarose?'

'Yes.'

Zoya stood in front of the officer. She was scruffy, red, and trembling.

'Come here, sweetheart,' he said, gently. 'We need you to accompany us to the airbase and answer some questions. Reckon you're up to that?'

Zoya looked at Mr Maxim, who nodded. 'O-Of course.'

'Good,' said the officer. He patted his pockets to make sure he had everything. 'We need to get up there straight away. The sooner the better. Thank you, sir.'

He laid an arm on Zoya's shoulder and turned again to Mr Maxim. 'Questioning shouldn't take long. If you'd like to drop into the airbase in an hour she should be ready for collection.'

With that, the officers ushered Zoya away from the crowd and down the side of the orphanage where she'd seen Mr Whycherley's body. The reminder hit her hard, and she was only vaguely aware of her surroundings as the soldiers led her towards an alcove in the corner of the alley.

'Just wait there a second while we grab the transporter.'

Zoya did as she was told, happy to stand still and not think. She watched the officer in charge walk away, and barely noticed the other step into position behind her. Only when she felt a muscular forearm around her throat and found her face covered with a foul-smelling cloth did Zoya realize she'd made a big, big mistake.

Then everything went black.

7

When she woke, Zoya was enveloped in darkness. For a brief second, she felt like she was tucked up in bed at the orphanage, and she rolled over and reached down to pull up her blanket. It was at this point she noticed she wasn't under a blanket, and that her bed felt a lot harder than usual, and colder. 'Hmm.'

No sooner had the sound left Zoya's mouth than the day's events flooded back——the museum, the crowd at the orphanage, Mr Whycherley, the kidnapping. A wave of panic swept over her as she recalled the attack in the alley. Those Aviation Army soldiers, those . . . *whoever they were*, had kidnapped her. She shot her hand to her chest to check her locket was still there and felt the familiar lump beneath her shirt. *At least I've still got you.*

Creak.

Zoya lay still. She breathed slowly in the dark and tried to take stock. Wherever she was, she didn't want to be there. Whoever those men were, she didn't want to be with them.

That meant escape. And that meant using her brain. She engaged her senses and tried to work it out.

Creak.

That was it! The sound was so rhythmic, so constant she'd barely noticed it. But it was there, in the background. And there was a rocking movement too.

Creak-crawk-creak-crawk.

'Strange.'

Quietly, in case the Aviation Army soldiers who'd kidnapped her were outside the room, she dropped to the floor. Her eyes had adjusted somewhat to the darkness now, and she was able to make out a little more of her surroundings. It appeared to be made from wood, and was empty aside from a cleaning mop discarded in one corner and a heating pipe built into another. Scurrying across the floor, illuminated by a shaft of light creeping through a crack on the other side of the room, were hundreds of tiny bugs. Zoya shuddered.

She proceeded to work her way around the edge of the room, running her hands up and down the walls, searching for the door. She found it a minute later and felt around for the handle. When she located it, a mixture of fear and excitement swelled inside of her. She gulped a breath of stale air and forced herself to continue. Grasping the handle, she turned it—just a tiny twist—to see if it would move.

It didn't.

Of course they wouldn't kidnap you just to leave you in an unlocked room!

Zoya rummaged in her back pocket. Buried beneath a handful of coins and paper scraps was the bent pin she'd used to unlock Mr Whycherley's desk drawer. 'Now we're talking.'

Thirty seconds later, the lock was open. As she slid the pin back into her pocket, Zoya considered what she was about to do. If she opened the door and escaped, she'd likely run into her kidnappers. On the other hand, if she remained they'd come for her sooner or later anyway. And who knew what they had planned? If they were the same people who'd killed Mr Whycherley . . .

She twisted the handle.

A cold rush of air hit Zoya in the face. Directly ahead stood a wall of crates twice her height. To her right, the view trailed into darkness. And to her left, all she could see was the moon.

Another gust of wind blew across her neck and she flicked open her jacket collar. The wind surged down the tunnel, howling in her ears, making her feel more afraid than she already was. There were other sounds too, clanking metal and creaking floorboards. From somewhere nearby she heard a flapping noise, and further off the gruff shout of a man.

Zoya backed up against the crates and started to creep down the passage, listening for sounds that might have been made by a person. After a while, a T-junction emerged out of the gloom——one arm formed by her cell, the other by the crates. Beyond, the route was blocked by a shoulder-high wall. Zoya glanced past this to see if she could make anything out, but all she could see was darkness. It was as if the world dropped away.

Puzzled, she tiptoed to the junction and poked her head around the corner to check the new passage was clear. Satisfied, she approached the wall and scrambled up so she could see over the top. So startled was she by what she saw that she let go of the wall and dropped to the floor. She sat there for a few moments, staring at the wood, then pulled herself back up to check she wasn't imagining things. 'It can't be . . .'

Zoya scanned the length of the wall, which stretched as far as she could see in both directions. It was then that the reality of her situation dawned on her, the cold truth. All that wind, the creaking wood, the flapping——it all made sense now. She understood why her kidnappers hadn't bothered to tie her hands, why they hadn't locked her in a more secure room. There was no point. Even though Zoya had escaped her cell, she was still a prisoner and would be until her kidnappers decided otherwise. Zoya DeLarose was over a mile high, riding the waves of the sky. She was trapped on a gigantic airship.

8

Zoya's heart thumped so fast she couldn't feel the breaks between beats. This was matched by her breathing, which fluttered in and out, the cold freezing her lungs. In the distance, the moon shone crisp against the black sky, surrounded by a swell of clouds that extended down to the ship—dark blue and silver baubles with wandering wisps.

An airship! Zoya opened her mouth in shock.

The craft reminded her of those she'd seen in Garibald Amstad's museum—curved, wooden galleons with mazes of walkways, lookout pods, sails, deck, and quarters. And yet this one was so, so much bigger. From her position next to what she now realized was the airship's gunwale, she could see the central deck, punctuated by three enormous masts, each as wide as her body and adorned by webs of silvery netting and wooden pods. Huge, white sails unfurled from these, all tied together and billowing in the evening wind, slapping against the wood. Beyond, the ship curved away into fog. Zoya could still make out the basic shape of the airship's bridge near the stern—a squat, square platform preceded by a run of steps. On top of this, its brass shining even at night, was the airship's wheel. Beside Zoya was a horseshoe of buildings, one arm formed by her cell. Further down the deck to her right—past the buildings—the port and starboard sides of the ship started to come together to form the prow, its figurehead soaring up and out so that it stood almost as high off the deck as the lowest sails. In spite of its majesty, the airship was a crumbling old thing.

Whumph.

A door slammed down the passage. Zoya was up and moving before she had time to blink. To her left, wedged up against the wall, was a line of barrels. She leapt for them like a tiger and landed in between them and the gunwale. Immediately, she swivelled on her toes so she was ready to pounce. Zoya held her breath as her heart continued to pound, and waited.

A full minute elapsed before she allowed herself a peek. In the distance, a man thrust a lantern into crags and corners of the ship. He made his way along the line of crates Zoya had edged down earlier, kicking one every now and then when he thought he'd spied something, before disappearing around the corner and out of sight. Zoya let go of her breath for the first time in a minute. 'I need to get out of here.'

The only other crew member on deck was a boy a year or two younger than Zoya. She spotted him sitting in one of the lookout pods that branched off the mainmast, tossing a pair of binoculars up and down and chatting away to a cat that had joined him. It was whilst trying to work out what such a friendly-looking boy was doing with the kidnappers that Zoya first spotted the parachutes.

There were three in total, tossed over a wooden crossbeam. Zoya recognized them from the museum, which meant they had to be pretty old. Indeed, the material of the canopy bags was frayed, and the cords looked worn. Still, they were her golden ticket out of there. Rather take her chance with a parachute than see what the kidnappers had planned.

Zoya groped around on the floor for something to throw. There was nothing at her feet, but she noticed one of the barrels had its stopper turned towards her. If she could wrench it out, throw it behind the boy, wait for him to investigate, then run up and grab a chute, she could strap it on and jump to freedom.

Zoya grasped the plug with both hands and tugged. At first it seemed fixed, but with a bit of wriggling and a few more tugs it started to loosen. Eventually it came away. For a few seconds, she watched the boy play with the cat, waiting for him to glance away, turn around, or do *something* to give her an opening. In the end, the cat came to her rescue, spotting Zoya in her hiding place and starting to meow to get her attention.

'What are you mewing at?' asked the boy, spinning in his pod.

Zoya sensed her chance. She gave the plug an almighty toss and watched it arc through the air before it clattered into a metal hook a yard above the boy's head. Instantly, he cast his head up and peered at the hook, trying to work out what had made the noise.

Zoya burst out from behind the barrels and sprinted towards the parachutes. As she moved, she determined which was the least wrecked, leapt into the air and tugged at it. At first the bag caught on the beam, but with a few yanks Zoya was able to loosen it. She stood, arms raised beneath the falling chute, praying she'd catch it before it thudded to the deck. The bag landed in her arms before she could even finish the thought, and she spun on her heels and pumped her legs, slinging the pack on her back and bolting back to her hiding place.

There, she adjusted the parachute so it sat comfortably on her shoulders, then tightened the straps. She took the canopy cord in her hand and gave it a pull. It seemed OK. Zoya poked her head above the barrels and scoured the passage for somewhere to jump. Halfway along was a break in the wood. It was small, but it would have to do.

After checking the way was clear, Zoya crawled to the gap and wedged herself in. If she was ever going to escape, it had to be now. She tugged the straps of her parachute one last time, then leaned over the edge of the airship. For a short way, the hull ran straight down, then it curved inwards and away. Beyond, was sky. Way down, a mile or so below, she made out the faint orange smudge of a city at night. It looked beautiful and warm against the black. *Guess that's what I'll aim for.*

Zoya closed her eyes and stepped off the airship. A silent scream escaped her mouth. It continued for a few seconds before Zoya realized that free-falling from an airship wasn't half as bad as she'd thought. Indeed, it was peaceful. There was no wind whipping past her cheeks, no roaring sound as she cut through the atmosphere. Just peace and quiet.

Zoya opened her eyes.

Something was wrong. The ghostly night-time clouds floated along in exactly the same formations as before, and the hull was still at her back. She looked to her left, then her right. Nothing. It was only when she looked above her that Zoya saw what had to be the biggest man on the planet. His arm, bigger than Zoya's waist, was clamped around the straps of her parachute.

9

'Captain,' said the big man a few minutes later. He dumped Zoya into an old leather chair.

'Thank you, Beebee,' said another voice, although Zoya couldn't locate its owner. Beebee lobbed Zoya's parachute into the corner of the room, flashed Zoya a toothy smile, and let himself out.

Zoya looked around. She'd been brought to a large, lavishly-decorated room overflowing with antique clocks, bookcases, sofas, and enough paintings to fill a gallery. Providing illumination were a handful of oil lanterns, giving the room a dream-like quality. Next to Zoya's parachute was a solid dining table, littered with the crumbs of a thousand meals, and in the opposite corner a writing desk, equally food-stained. However, neither piece of furniture was the room's centrepiece. That honour went to a mechanical skymap resting on a plinth in the middle of the room. A single glance told Zoya it was the most detailed map she'd ever seen. It spanned the entire globe and pinpointed every mountain, river, ocean, and city. She stood to take a closer look.

'Quite something, eh?'

This time Zoya caught the direction of the voice and flicked her head. Seated near the writing desk, his body and face obscured by shadow, was a man. Zoya squinted into the gloom. The man was leaning back, studying her. He wore a sturdy pair of leather boots that matched a black waistcoat and white shirt. Cropped salt-and-pepper hair framed bushy eyebrows and a tidy moustache. When he noticed Zoya had spotted him, he stirred in his seat, causing a dagger strapped to his side to *thunk* against the wood. 'Don't be afraid,' he said, 'you're safe here.'

Zoya didn't respond. Instead, she charged the man with all her might, barrelling into his midriff. 'What do you want?' she shouted between punches. 'I hate you! You killed Mr Whycherley! What do you want?'

All the fury inside of Zoya erupted. She pounded the man with her fists, giving little thought to the dagger at his side. He allowed Zoya to beat his chest and arms until she was red in the face and collapsed to the floor. Then he picked her up and carried her back to the leather chair. He walked to his desk.

'I hope you feel somewhat better having done that, Zoya DeLarose.' He straightened his clothes. 'You've had a rough few hours. But mark my words, that's the last time you lay your hands on me or one of my crew. Understand?'

Zoya examined him through bleary eyes. 'Who are you?'

'My name,' said the man, 'is Carlos Manuel Vaspine. And we need to talk.'

10

Zoya didn't speak. Not only was she exhausted from the attack, but there was something about the man that made her want to listen. Vaspine walked to the table beside which Beebee, the big man, had dumped Zoya's parachute. He nodded towards the chute. 'Good job Beebee caught you. Those things had their cords removed months ago. We needed them to tie up prisoners. You'd have landed like a pancake.'

Zoya frowned.

'Zoya,' continued Vaspine, noting that his attempt at humour had failed, 'do you know where you are?'

'I'm with the man who killed Mr Whycherley.'

Vaspine shot her a glance. 'Watch who you're accusing, young lady. Richard Whycherley was a friend of mine. His death cuts me deeply.'

Zoya stared. If he was telling the truth—if this man's people weren't responsible for killing Mr Whycherley—who were they? And why had they kidnapped her?

'In fact,' continued Vaspine, 'mine and Richard's friendship is the reason you're here now. Now, *do* you know where you are?'

Zoya's only clue was the soldiers who'd kidnapped her. 'Is this an Aviation Army airship?'

Vaspine scoffed. 'Those buffoons? They couldn't rescue a monkey from a zoo.'

'The men who kidnapped me were wearing army uniforms,' said Zoya.

'You should be wary of judging situations by what you see alone,' said Vaspine. 'I sent my men down dressed as soldiers for a reason. How do you think two sky thieves would have fared at a guarded murder scene without disguise?'

The words sky thieves entered Zoya's ears, but their meaning didn't register right away. Though she'd read about thieves all her life, and played sky-thief games every break, she never thought she'd be sat with a captain in his quarters. She exploded from her seat. 'You're a sky thief?'

'Everyone on this ship is,' said Vaspine. 'So, too, will you be, for a while.'

Zoya's smile faded. 'You mean I'm a prisoner?'

'Let's just say you won't be leaving this ship for a while. Right now, it's not safe.'

'And I *am* safe here?' said Zoya. 'With sky thieves? You're the most dangerous people on the planet.'

'And how would you know that?'

'Everybody knows.'

Vaspine smiled. 'I suppose most pirates do give us a bad name. But remember what I said about judging things too hastily. Not all of us are what we're made out to be.'

A moment's silence passed, punctuated by the crackling of oil lanterns. Vaspine stared at Zoya. 'Tell me, Miss DeLarose, have you heard of the *Dragonfly*?'

Zoya had. The *Dragonfly* was one of the only thief airships Mr Whycherley spoke positively about. The thieves of the *Dragonfly* didn't brawl, they didn't kill. They only robbed airships that could afford it, and gave every penny to those in need, those desperate for food, clothes, or a roof over their heads.

'You weren't on the *Dragonfly*?' she said.

'On her?' laughed Vaspine. He rose from his seat and gestured at everything about him. 'I own the damn thing!'

11

Zoya gazed around the room. 'This is the *Dragonfly*?'

Vaspine nodded. 'Don't be too impressed, though. She might look magnificent, but she's falling apart on the inside.' He brushed a hand along a nearby wall. 'But enough of this. Tell me what you know of the *White Knight*.'

Zoya shrugged, puzzled. 'Not much. Just what we learned at the orphanage.'

Vaspine rose from his seat and parted his hands in the air as if unfurling an imaginary banner. 'The scourge of the skies. The terror supreme.' He shook his head. 'It's all false. That ship wasn't a scourge, as the Aviation Army wants everyone to believe. It was run by two of the kindest people I've ever met.'

'Jupiter and Dominika . . .' said Zoya.

Vaspine nodded, impressed.

'But they're two of the worst pirates in history,' protested Zoya. 'They killed hundreds!'

'Not so,' said Vaspine. 'They never killed a soul.'

'How do you know?'

'Because,' said Vaspine, inhaling deeply, 'I was with them when they were supposed to be doing it.'

Zoya laughed nervously. 'You . . . you served on the *White Knight?*'

'Me and a man called Lendon Kane. We were Jupiter's lieutenants.'

'What were they like?'

'Jupiter and Dominika?' Vaspine considered the question. 'Good people. Gentle, kind. They were like us. They never robbed for their own benefit. And they didn't hurt anyone.'

Zoya frowned. 'I've heard of Kane.' An image of the pyramid of pirates at Garibald Amstad's Fabulous World of Flying Machines entered her mind. 'You can't tell me he was gentle.'

'You're right, he's the devil.'

'So, what happened?'

Vaspine sighed. 'For a long time, things were fine. Then Dominika had a child and after that Jupiter never left the ship. He considered raids too dangerous for a man with a baby. He put me and Kane in charge. Everything carried on as normal at first, but then I noticed a change in Kane. He seemed to get a little rougher with the people we robbed, knocking them about. He ordered everyone to carry weapons.

'And he hated the way Jupiter gave away our swag. Kane needled the men about it behind his back. Jupiter knew, but he let it slide. Big mistake. Kane worked on the men for months. He whipped them into such a storm that he was able to convince them to mutiny.'

Zoya shifted in her chair.

'He'd planned it for weeks. The first I knew was when Jupiter and Dominika came to my quarters late one night with the baby. I'd never seen Jupiter so shaken. He told me about the mutiny, and how Kane had killed the men who disagreed, and how all the rest were searching the airship for Jupiter to finish the job.

'I told him we should fight. He said that's what he was going to do. But not me. He had another job for me. He pulled out a locket, bundled it into a blanket, wrapped that around his baby and handed them to me. "Take them somewhere safe," he said. "You'll choose the right place. I'm going to end this."

'I argued, of course. I was the best swordsman on the ship, better even than Jupiter. I knew he needed me. But he and Dominika insisted, they told me to get away. So I did. I jumped into the transporter, fled to the surface and dropped off the baby at an orphanage. When I got back to where I'd left the *White Knight*, it was gone. I searched and searched, but it was no use. I drifted down to the surface to decide what to do. A few days later, I heard gossip that Kane and his men had simply overwhelmed Jupiter and Dominika. They murdered them in cold blood.'

There was a long pause after Vaspine finished his story. Zoya watched the captain gaze silently into the room.

'What about the baby?' asked Zoya.

'You're not stupid, Zoya. You know damn well about the baby.'

'Say it, please. So I know I've got it right.'

Vaspine looked at her. 'Zoya, that baby was you.'

12

Zoya shook her head.

'Yes,' said Vaspine. 'I put you there myself. I've been checking on you all these years.'

'My parents were . . .'

Vaspine nodded.

'Why didn't you come and get me?'

'You were safe at the orphanage. I never told anyone where I'd taken you and I knew I could trust Richard Whycherley. There was no way Kane would find you there.'

'Find me?' Zoya sat up straight. 'Why would he want to find me?'

Vaspine opened his mouth to speak, then hesitated. When he spoke again, his eyes bore into Zoya's. 'Zoya, you need to understand this man. He's merciless. And you're Jupiter's last living relative. Of course he searched for you.'

'But why did he kill Mr Whycherley?'

'Richard must have confronted him when he broke in. God knows how Kane found you, but you were lucky you were out. I'm surprised he didn't get you anyway. My men told me he was there when they picked you up.'

Zoya thought back to those minutes outside the orphanage. An image of the man in black burst into her mind. 'What does he look like?'

Vaspine tilted his head. 'Tall, slim, black hair. Moustache. Oh, and he wears a top hat . . .'

'I saw him!' said Zoya. 'He was watching me outside the orphanage.'

'Then we've been luckier than I thought. Those Aviation Army buffoons, by their very presence alone, might just have saved your life.' The captain blinked tiredly, then rubbed his eyes. 'Right, for now you stay on the *Dragonfly*. God knows we couldn't hold off Kane's ship if it came—no ship in the sky can match the *Shadow*. But there's nowhere safer.'

'How do I know you're not Kane?' asked Zoya, suddenly. 'After all, you're the one that kidnapped me. How do I know this isn't a trick?'

Vaspine shrugged. 'You don't. But right now I'm the only game in town.' The captain walked to his cabin window, parted the blinds and glanced into the courtyard. When he returned, his eyes were pensive. 'Having said that, you might've stumbled on something there, Zoya. Old ships like this have wide ears and loose tongues. It would be wise to keep your past a secret for now.'

'What if someone asks?'

'Tell the truth,' said Vaspine. 'Or, at least, some of it.' He crossed to the corner of his room, retrieved a broom and handed it to her. 'Tell them you're an orphan we picked up from the surface to work on the ship. A cleaner. Elaborate. Just, whatever you do, don't mention your parents, or Kane, or,' he signalled towards Zoya's neck, 'the locket.'

Zoya stood up. She looked at the captain. 'Am I going to be OK?'

'You might,' he said, 'if you follow my instructions and give me time to think. Now, I suggest you get out of here before people realize there's something wrong. Beebee's outside, he'll show you where to sleep.'

Zoya walked towards the door.

'Not a word to anyone, Zoya.'

She nodded.

Beebee remained quiet as Zoya emerged, pushing himself off a metal grate and ducking beneath the wooden arch that led to the rest of the ship. Zoya followed, past her makeshift prison and down a narrow tunnel. Off to one side was a den, framed by wooden planks and covered by old rugs. Illuminating the scene was a single oil lantern. 'Is that it?' asked Zoya.

Beebee gestured towards the gap at the front of the den, then left. 'Well, it's either this or the cell. And that cell leaks like a watering can. Your choice.'

Zoya watched him disappear, sighed, then lifted the overhanging rug and crawled inside.

Outside, the wind still blew hard, tossing the fabric above her head and spraying water from where it had collected. Stretched across the floor was a section of carpet, this thinner than the rugs. It was dark, but the little light highlighted stains. Piled in the corner was a straw duvet, coated with a layer of dust so thick it made Zoya shudder. She gathered up the duvet, shook it onto the deck outside, then stretched out on the carpet and dragged it over her. As she lay shivering, she listened to the whirr of the airship and the *pitter-patter* of rain. The ship seemed louder than it had from her cell, bigger. For an hour Zoya tossed and turned, trying to sleep. She thought about Jupiter, Kane, Captain Vaspine, her locket. After a while, her eyes started to grow heavy, then heavier, until, like a candle being snuffed out by the wind, she drifted off for her first night's sleep on an airship.

13

The sun was shining by the time Zoya emerged from her den. It was accompanied by an early morning breeze that blew over the hull and buffeted her tent. Outside, a storm of people swirled, each with a job and a determined look that convinced Zoya it would get done. There were around a dozen in total, dressed in ripped trousers, tattered jumpers, and cotton waistcoats. One or two had tattoos on their hands and necks. Zoya walked into the centre of the maelstrom, weaving to avoid bumping into people. She half-expected everyone to stop what they were doing and stare at her, but for the most part they just ignored her. The only person to speak to Zoya was an old lady with an armful of mops who needed her to get out of the way.

Zoya hopped aside, then stumbled to avoid another thief approaching from the opposite direction. When she regained her footing, she found herself at the edge of the airship, near to where she'd tried to jump the previous evening. In the dark, everything had looked spooky, scary. In the daylight, the ship and everything around it looked majestic. All the space, the empty sky, made Zoya feel like she was on a Ferris wheel at the top of the world. She watched the ship's prow slice through the clouds, before leaning over the starboard gunwale and looking down to the ground. The night before she'd seen faint orange blurs. Now the landscape was a patchwork of mountains, rivers, lakes, forests, and fields. Below the ship, a formation of birds banked left and right, mirroring the *Dragonfly*.

It was whilst watching the birds that Zoya earned her first sky thief insult. 'Oi! Big ears!'

She heard the voice, but had no idea where it came from. She searched around, half-expecting to see Captain Vaspine or Beebee.

'Hello?' called Zoya.

'Up here.'

Zoya followed the direction of the voice to a position a few feet above her head. A boy was sitting on a wooden beam. Once he was certain she'd seen him, he rolled backwards off the beam, spun in mid-air and landed on his feet on the deck. Zoya recognized him as the lad she'd seen in the lookout the previous evening. He eyed her warily.

He was a funny-looking kid, Zoya decided. Slightly younger than her, he wore a pair of scuffed, black trousers beneath a worn pale-blue shirt. Holding up the trousers were a pair of orange braces, one frayed at the end. He had a slim face perched atop a tanned, lean body, and he stared at Zoya from beneath a tangle of fawn hair. 'That was a mean trick you played last night,' he said. He bounced Zoya's stopper between his hands. 'I found it this morning.' He flung the stopper at Zoya. It ricocheted off and landed on the deck.

'Sorry.' Zoya shrugged. 'I needed to distract you.'

'Mean,' continued the boy. 'I ought to give you a whack, coming onto my ship and causing trouble.'

Zoya grimaced in apology.

'Why are you still here anyway?' asked the boy. He glanced at the nearby pirates, then back at Zoya. 'Why hasn't the captain thrown you overboard like every other stowaway?'

Based on her meeting with the captain, Zoya doubted this. But she remained quiet. Her silence prompted the boy to step forward. 'You got me in trouble last night.'

'You shouldn't be so easy to trick then.'

The boy opened his mouth to speak, then closed it. There was an edge to his voice when he finally spoke. 'Why are you here, anyway?' He lunged forwards and shoved her in the chest. 'You come to my ship.' Shove. 'Get me in trouble.' Shove. 'Then you come here and get cheeky.' Shove. Zoya skipped back with each push, trying to deflect the boy's arms. But with each retreat, her own blood boiled a little hotter. Images of Mr Whycherley and the orphanage fused with the boy's face, until all she could see was flames. She waited for the boy to raise his hands again, then grabbed

48

his wrists and twisted hard. Without releasing her grip, she swung him off to the side, bashing him into a mast. As he slumped to the deck, Zoya looked about to see who'd seen. There were still a few thieves nearby, although most seemed too preoccupied to have noticed. Zoya returned her attention to the boy, who was holding one of his braces, which had torn against the mast. His face registered confusion, then rage. He burst towards Zoya in a whirlwind of fists, to which Zoya replied with her own, jabbing his arms and chest. Soon, they were rolling on the floor, wrestling, trying to gain top position. This continued for thirty seconds—Zoya taking a couple of hard blows and dealing a few of her own—before they heard an almighty shout over their shoulders. 'Stop!'

Zoya and the boy froze.

'Just what the hell do you think you're doing?'

Zoya untangled her arms from the boy's and pushed him away. Across the deck was an old man, his arms locked to his hips and bushy eyebrows furrowed in a sharp 'v'. Surrounding him were a number of other thieves, all having stopped what they were doing to stare at the children.

'If the captain saw this he'd have your guts on a plate,' said the old man. 'Fighting on the *Dragonfly*. I've seen it all!'

Zoya glanced at the boy, whose sunken eyes registered embarrassment. 'I was just . . .'

'Oh, here we go,' said the old man, folding his arms, 'because if I'm not much mistaken, you got in trouble last night for leaving your station. Let's hear your excuse this time . . .'

Zoya climbed to her feet and dusted down her clothes. 'I asked him for help.'

The man stopped mid-sentence. 'I beg your pardon.'

'I asked him for help.'

The man held Zoya's stare. 'Did you now? And are you this newcomer I've been hearing about?'

Zoya nodded. 'I was lost, so I asked him.'

'I see.' The old man looked her up and down. 'Well, a rule you'll learn on our ship, missy, is that you don't distract other thieves when they're working. You'll do well to remember that.'

Zoya smiled. 'I will.'

'Very well,' said the old man. He took one last look at the boy, shook his head, then whirled his hand in a gesture for the others to get back to work. Zoya waited for them to leave, then put out her hand for the boy. He stared at it, eyeing Zoya with suspicion, then extended his own.

'I am sorry for last night,' said Zoya. 'And I'm sorry for . . .' she nodded down at a bruise forming on the boy's arm.

The boy gazed at his fists, then up at a matching bruise on the side of Zoya's cheek. 'And I'm sorry for . . .' he paused, '. . . that.' Zoya smiled as the boy tucked the torn end of his brace into his shirt. 'The old fellow was right, wasn't he?' said the boy. 'You're new?'

Zoya nodded.

'What's your name?'

'Zoya DeLarose.'

'Well, I'm Bucker Blake,' said the boy. 'And I guess I owe you one. Do you want to come up to the crow's nest? I'll show you around.'

'Sure,' said Zoya. 'How do we get up?'

Bucker looked at her like she'd dropped her brain off the side of the airship. 'Climb, dummy!' And with that, he bolted in the direction of the nearest mast.

14

By the time Zoya reached the bottom of the pole, Bucker had already climbed up to the cross-beam that linked the ship's lookouts. Zoya followed as best she could, but still trailed behind.

'Come on,' called Bucker. 'I've seen snails move faster!'

When they reached the mainmast, a race started to reach the uppermost platform. Zoya hauled herself up the rigging two rungs at a time, determined to demonstrate her speed. But by that point Bucker had built up such a lead that not even a spider on its web would have caught him. When she eventually made it up—panting and gulping down air—he gave her a pitying smile. 'If you want me to carry you next time, just ask.'

The platform sat on top of the mainmast like ice cream on a cone. It seemed to serve no purpose other than as somewhere for the crew to go when they wanted a bit of peace. Once Zoya was safely positioned on the wooden planks, she too felt content. The breeze blowing through her hair reminded her of similar days on the roof of the orphanage.

'It's a bit tight,' said Bucker, budging her over.

'I guess.'

'All these instruments used to belong to the Doc.' Bucker gestured at the telescopes and measuring devices scattered around. 'He was the ship's scientist. Left a year or so ago. Smartest man in the world,' Bucker winked. 'Or so he said. Grumpy old man's more like it.'

He tossed Zoya a pair of binoculars and motioned for her to use them. Zoya set them to her eyes the wrong way at first, and Bucker had to jab her in the side to correct her. 'Where did they get you?'

From their position atop the mainmast, Zoya could see the entire airship. The crew, still scurrying about performing their morning work, looked like ants.

'Right,' said Bucker, grabbing another pair of binoculars, 'let me tell you who's who. You've met the most important person already, of course.'

'The captain.'

'Me, you idiot! Although the captain's pretty important too, I guess.'

Zoya chuckled.

'After that, you've got to get in with Cid Lightfoot,' said Bucker. 'He's the pilot.'

Bucker pointed to the ship's stern. Standing on a raised platform was a tall, athletic man with shoulder-length, sun-bleached hair held in place by a red bandana. Over a white T-shirt he wore an aviator's brown leather jacket that reminded Zoya of the antiques she'd seen in Garibald Amstad's museum. In one of his hands he was tossing a gold coin, whilst the other was fixed to the ship's wheel.

'Can you see him shouting?' asked Bucker.

Zoya could. Indeed, he'd been roaring at a petrified crew member the entire time.

'He's actually nice,' said Bucker. 'He just gets a little stressed when he's flying. So says Mum, anyway.'

'Where's your mum?'

'She,' said Bucker, tucking his legs to his chin and spinning on his backside, 'is there.' He pointed in the direction of a heavy-set lady of about forty, leaning against the wall of crates Zoya had hidden behind the previous evening. Before her, a couple of thieves practised fencing.

'Your mum teaches sword-fighting?' asked Zoya, impressed.

'Rosie Blake, she's the best in the sky!'

Zoya watched her snatch a sword from one of her student's hands and make a series of slashing motions towards the other. The second student dropped his sword to the deck and shook his head in amazement.

Zoya turned to Bucker. 'What about Beebee?'

'Beebee?' said Bucker. 'He's my best friend on the entire ship.'

He moved onto his belly so he could lean his head over

the edge of the platform. Zoya did the same, ignoring the queasy feeling in her stomach. She spotted Beebee below, trying to play with a bird that had landed near the port gunwale. The bird, perhaps worried it was about to become part of a stew, fluttered back every time Beebee stepped forwards. The look of puzzlement on the big man's face made Bucker giggle. He nodded at Beebee. 'Just wait until you see him fighting.'

Beebee was enormous, even bigger than Zoya had judged the previous evening. His head was as big as her torso, and on it he wore a thick, ribbed beanie hat. His huge biceps threatened to tear open his white T-shirt at the armholes. 'That right?' she said.

'Yeah,' said Bucker. 'He could crush most people's skulls with one hand. And he's a champion boxer. Won every fight he ever entered.'

'Cool.' Zoya lifted her binoculars for another look, but as she did she noticed something on the horizon. At first, she thought it was another airship breaking through the clouds, but then she realized that if it was an airship it had to be one with a covering of snow. Something about that seemed wrong. She pointed the shape out to Bucker. 'What's that?'

Bucker turned from where he'd been jabbing at one of the Doc's instruments and peered through his binoculars. His face froze when he realized what he was seeing. 'Oh my God,' he whimpered. 'Not again. Cid's going to kill me!'

'What's going on?' asked Zoya.

'Do you see that black bit at the top?'

'No,' said Zoya.

'Exactly.' Bucker edged backwards off the platform and started to make his way down the netting. 'Listen, sorry about the fight. It's been nice meeting you, come and see me again!'

With that, Zoya lost sight of him amongst the sails. She raised the binoculars to get another look at the object. This time, Zoya's stomach shot to her throat. Ahead of the ship, growing by the second, was a mountain. Except where there should have been a peak was instead an ocean of fiery orange. *Oh wow*, thought Zoya, nearly falling off the platform, *a volcano*.

15

Zoya dashed from the platform and started to half-climb, half-fall down the rigging. She burned her palms trying to keep up with Bucker, who was already far below. Halfway down, Zoya stopped to look at the volcano, which had grown significantly since she'd last seen it. From its puckered caldera, the mountain spewed vast smoky plumes that drifted towards the ship, obscuring Zoya's view. She judged they had about a minute before they hit the smoke, and another before the airship smashed into the rock.

Zoya sped up her descent and reached the deck, her heart pounding and her hands raw. She searched around for Bucker, who was already up the other end of the ship, sprinting towards Cid. With nowhere else to go, she followed.

Bucker was shouting when Zoya arrived. '. . . over there, a volcano!'

Cid eyed the boy as if he'd heard the joke before and wasn't in the mood to hear it again. But when Bucker didn't move, his face sagged. Immediately, he pocketed his pipe and squinted into the distance. His face turned white. He lifted a pair of binoculars to his eyes and stared for another few seconds—his brow furrowing as he studied the scene—before he dropped the lenses and turned back to Bucker. 'You left it late this time, kid!'

Before Bucker could respond, Cid turned away and started issuing orders. 'Increase speed!' he yelled. 'Get that sail to full mast!'

Once he'd spurred everyone to action, the pilot returned to Bucker. 'Right, you'd better find Beebee within the next thirty seconds or we'll all be eating lava for lunch!'

Bucker shot off towards the bow, leaving Zoya alone with Cid. She watched to see what the pilot would do next, but he didn't move. Instead, he leaned against the ship's wheel and stared at the volcano, which grew by the second. Zoya felt like running up to him, shaking him, shouting at him to do something! It took every ounce of her control not to spring up and grab the wheel.

'Why aren't we changing course?' she blurted.

Cid swung his head slowly in her direction. 'In about ten seconds, this ship is going to hit hot air. When it does, everything on this hunk of wood is going to start shaking like a tambourine. If there were ten of you and ten of me, we still wouldn't be strong enough to hold that wheel. There's only one person on this airship who is . . .' Cid glanced over Zoya's shoulder, '. . . and he's here now.'

Zoya swung around. Sprinting up the ship was Bucker, followed by Beebee, Vaspine, and Bucker's mother.

'I found him,' Bucker said, as he arrived.

'Good lad.' Cid turned to Beebee. 'Beebee, get on the wheel and pull as hard as you can.'

'Which direction?'

'Any!'

Beebee started to move. Cid grabbed the big man's arm as he passed. 'Whatever you do, hold on!'

Beebee stepped into position behind the wheel as Vaspine and Rosie arrived.

'What's going on?' asked the captain.

'I hope you've brought some sausages,' said Cid, nodding over the captain's shoulder, 'because it's about to get mighty hot up here.'

Vaspine turned around. The volcano loomed ahead, its peak belching angry smoke into the sky. Vaspine turned back and grinned at Beebee. 'Hold on, son.'

Beebee slammed his hands onto the wheel just as the first blast of hot air hit. It jolted the ship like an earthquake, tossing people like dolls. Only Beebee managed to hold his ground, gripping the wheel in his massive hands and hauling the spokes around. Eventually, the wheel locked at its outermost point, and Beebee leaned in to stop it jerking back, his muscles bulging beneath his skin.

As the ship drifted towards the volcano, it became more

unstable, bucking Zoya and the rest of the crew. Zoya was lucky to find herself slammed up against one of the smaller masts, and she shot out her arms to grab it. When she had a good grip, she sidestepped around until she could see the volcano. Individual boulders were visible on its slope now, and Zoya could feel its heat burning her forehead. There was a smell of sulphur, too, so strong she had to remove a hand from the mast to cover her nose.

Back on the bridge, Beebee started to shake. A deep, rasping sound emanated from his throat every time he exhaled, and a vein at the side of his head throbbed like it was about to explode.

'Another ten seconds,' shouted Cid.

Beebee let out a roar so loud it made Bucker jump. He leaned into the wheel for one last push, every fibre in his body as firm as granite. Gradually, the ship started to turn away from the volcano and into the clear sky. As they put distance between the mountain and themselves, the buffeting began to ease. One by one, the crew members staggered to their feet. Only when Beebee knew they were safe did he let go of the wheel and collapse onto the floor. 'Next time,' he said to Bucker, through coughs, 'you tell me you have a surprise . . .'

'Yeah?'

'I'd prefer ice cream.'

16

It took most of the rest of the day to get the ship back to normal. Zoya spent the time buzzing between thieves, offering her help and trying to hide her frown when they said no. Every now and then, one would pity her as the new girl and invent a job for her. As she executed the task, Zoya would ask them about their lives on the ship, whilst doing her best to deflect any questions about her own.

By sunset, most of the smoke had been scrubbed from the decks, the fires quenched, the crockery returned to its cupboards, and the beds righted. Zoya headed inside with the rest of the crew for dinner, then wandered back onto the deck to meet more of the thieves. She chatted first with an ex-circus performer whose role on the *Dragonfly* was to contort his body and get into the smallest hiding places on the ships they robbed, then with a lady who bragged of having ten children back on the surface, and how she wanted each to own their own airship, '. . . just like the boss.'

Eventually, Zoya wandered to the bridge, where the excitement of the volcano had taken place. It was quiet now. The wheel—strained almost to snapping by Beebee—stood in the centre of the platform as if nothing had happened. Zoya crept up to it, imagining she was the captain of her own airship. She gripped a spoke either side and tested how far she could turn it.

'It's a lot easier without the volcano,' said a voice.

Behind Zoya, Beebee was sitting on the floor, his back up against the starboard gunwale. Beside him was a bottle of disinfectant which he applied to his shredded hands. Zoya walked over. 'They must hurt.'

'They've been worse.'

'That was pretty amazing, what you did.'

'It's easy when you're as big as me,' dismissed Beebee. 'Zoya, isn't it?'

Zoya nodded.

'You haven't been jumping off any more airships, have you?'

Zoya went crimson at the reminder. 'Thank you.'

'Don't mention it.'

Beebee finished applying the disinfectant to his grazes, then boosted himself off the deck and walked over to see if he'd done any damage to the wheel. 'I'm only sorry I had to grab you by the strap,' he continued. 'I could have broken your neck. Then again, you were stupid jumping off an airship, so I guess we're even.'

'Yeah,' agreed Zoya. She joined Beebee at the wheel. 'You know, of all the people on this ship, you're the one who looks most like the picture I had of a sky thief.'

'You mean big?'

'Yeah, and the muscles, the missing teeth, the tattoos.'

Beebee laughed. 'I suppose I do look pretty nasty compared to everyone else. You've got to remember though, the captain doesn't run a normal thief airship.' Beebee looked into the distance at another craft flying by. Zoya looked too. On top of the ship's mainmast was a black flag. 'A normal thief wouldn't last long with the captain.'

'How do *you*?'

Beebee laughed again, and he kept on laughing, making Zoya feel like she'd said something funny. 'I'm not as mean as I look,' he said, eventually. 'I might look like I've been scraped off the devil's boot, but I was taught to be good and fair when I was little, and good and fair I am.'

'What about your scars?'

Beebee paused to choose his words. 'Sometimes you have to fight for what's fair.'

17

'I saw you playing with the birds,' said Zoya.

Beebee rolled his eyes. 'You saw, huh? I've been trying to make friends with the little things, but they won't come near me. I've tried everything—standing, sitting, ignoring them, giving them treats—I've even tried smiling!' He grinned at Zoya, revealing a set of teeth so crooked that she understood why the birds might run. 'All I want is to hold one.'

Back at the orphanage, Mr Whycherley had been a keen ornithologist and it was often said he knew more about birds than the birds themselves. He kept a set of feeding tables in the orphanage gardens, and it had been one of Zoya's regular punishments to clean and refill them. So Zoya knew all about birds, and she was pretty sure she could teach Beebee how to make friends with the ones on the *Dragonfly*.

Zoya scanned the bridge to see if there were any nearby. The only bird she could see was a pigeon pecking around the deck behind the bridge. Zoya knew the pigeon's coo well, and she started to imitate it. The pigeon cocked its head and stared at Zoya. With their eyes locked, Zoya crept forwards until she was a foot away.

'Careful, he'll run—' began Beebee, but Zoya cut him off with the swipe of a hand. Her other, she laid flat on the deck, extended to the bird. The pigeon eyed it warily, before taking a few cautious steps forward. Zoya remained still and waited for the bird to take the few last steps, until it hopped onto her hand. Beebee looked down at the bird, then up at Zoya. 'How?' was all he could say.

'It's in the coo,' she whispered. 'I can teach you, but it takes a while.'

Beebee stepped towards the bird, but the movement was too sudden and the pigeon flapped away. They watched it dart off the side of the airship and into the sky. 'See what I mean?' said Beebee.

'You have to be gentle,' said Zoya.

'Gentle ain't my strong point. Listen, will you teach me how to do that, get a bird in my hand?'

'Definitely,' said Zoya. 'Maybe one day you can teach me how to fight?'

Beebee chuckled. 'I knew you were a brawler the minute I saw you. Go on then, if you can teach me, I'll make you the best boxer on the ship.' He winked. 'Apart from me, of course.'

'Of course,' agreed Zoya.

They chatted for a few more minutes, before Beebee excused himself and started to walk down the deck towards the crew's quarters. He'd made it as far as the bridge when he raised a finger and spun around. 'I almost forgot,' he said, 'the captain's managed to sort you a cabin. Do you want to see?'

Zoya recalled her previous night in the den and shivered. 'Yes please.'

Zoya followed Beebee along the deck, past a trio of pirates performing pull-ups on one of the cross-beams, then down towards the captain's quarters. Before he reached the passage that led to Vaspine, Beebee ducked under an archway, turned left, then stopped beside a low, wooden door. 'Here,' he said. 'Think you'll manage to navigate your way back to deck in the morning?'

Zoya smiled. 'I think so.'

Beebee bowed his head and vanished.

The room was welcoming enough. She poked around for a while and decided it had everything she might need — a bed, a table, a chair, a lamp and even a pile of books to read if she got bored.

For a few seconds, Zoya stood in the quiet, both excited and scared at the same time. Then her eyes started to droop. And faced with a bed that was, if not comfortable, at least a bed, she locked her door, kicked off her shoes, and slipped beneath the covers.

18

It took Zoya a while to get to sleep. She tossed and turned, at one point kicking her blanket to the floor, at another crawling off her bed to pick it up. Vaspine's story spun through her mind. She had so many questions about her mother and father. What were they like? How did they speak? How did they move? She thought of Kane, too. What if they couldn't escape him? What if he never gave up?

She eventually nodded off for a couple of hours before being woken in the middle of the night by a knocking on her door. She was unsure at first whether the sound was real or part of a dream, so she rolled over and ignored it. But when it came again—insistent, this time—she realized there really was someone outside. With eyes half-closed, she rolled out of bed and opened the door. 'Hello?'

Bucker stood in the passage, an irritated look on his face. 'Good job you answered that time,' he said, 'or I was about to get Beebee to knock it down.'

'Funny,' grumbled Zoya.

'I can see you're not an early bird,' said Bucker, arching his eyebrows. 'Listen, you need to get dressed. The captain wants you.'

'Me?'

'No, the king of the world. Yes, you!'

'What about?'

'Just get over there,' said Bucker.

Zoya dressed and followed Bucker as he scooted off towards Vaspine's quarters. She could tell by the full moon it was still the dead of night, and yet the ship seemed alive with activity. Thieves bustled—working the sails, carrying food, armour, weapons. Zoya noted everyone was dressed in black, and that apart from three dimmed lanterns, all the lights aboard were extinguished.

'What's going on?' she asked Beebee as he slipped by.

'Little bird lady!' said Beebee, but before Zoya could get anything out of him Bucker had tugged her arm and whisked her away. They arrived at Vaspine's quarters to find it crammed with people. As soon as the captain saw Zoya, he asked everyone apart from her and Rosie to leave.

'Good luck,' Vaspine shouted as everyone left.

'See you, Zoya,' said Bucker, closing the door.

Vaspine asked Zoya to sit. 'You've met Bucker's mother, haven't you?'

'Not properly.'

'I'm Rosie,' said the woman, offering her hand. 'Nice to meet you. Bucker's told me all about you.'

Vaspine perched on the desk in front of Zoya. 'Zoya, an opportunity's arisen. One that's too good to miss.'

'OK,' said Zoya, waiting for more.

'An airship's been spotted off the starboard side,' said Rosie. She walked to the window and parted the curtains. 'Have a look.'

Zoya walked over and looked to where Rosie was pointing. Far off in the distance she spied two parallel lines of faint, twinkling lights. They looked tiny from Vaspine's window, but if the ship was as distant as it appeared and Zoya could still see them, it had to be enormous!

'We don't get many chances like this,' continued Rosie. 'It's a cruiser, taking passengers on a tour around the world. There'll be a lot of rich people. The money we'll take will feed people on the surface for a year.'

'We're boarding tonight,' said Vaspine. 'In about ten minutes. I'm going to be leading the team. Ordinarily, a new recruit would come with us to learn the ropes. But seeing as you literally just joined I want you to man one of the lookouts instead . . .'

Zoya jumped up. 'No!'

'Excuse me?'

'I want to go.'

Vaspine glanced at Rosie who was still beside the window. She arched an eyebrow. 'Rosie,' said the captain, 'will you give us a moment?'

Rosie nodded, then smiled at Zoya and let herself out. When she was gone, Vaspine leaned in. 'Zoya, I'm not saving you from Kane just to put you in more danger.'

'But I need to go,' argued Zoya. 'If Kane comes and I've had no fighting experience, I'll be a sitting duck.'

Vaspine nodded at the faint lights through the window. 'It'll be dangerous. They might have security, Aviation Army. We know what we're doing, you don't.'

'But how will I ever learn?'

'You will. In time.'

Zoya racked her brain for a way to convince him, then threw up a finger. 'I can do things,' she said. 'I'm good at sneaking. And I can pick locks. I picked the one on the cell you put me in.'

Vaspine fixed her with a sidelong stare. Sensing she was getting through, Zoya searched the room for a lock to pick. The only object nearby was the captain's safe — a black, iron box resting on the floor beside his desk. Zoya crossed to this, bent to her knees and proceeded to pick its lock. After a minute, there was a *click* from somewhere near the back of the container, and the sound of a spring. The door opened.

The captain looked at her, then walked to the safe. He leaned down and studied the lock, running it under his fingers, his brain ticking over. Then he closed the door and snapped the lock back into place. He straightened his back and walked to his desk, deep in thought. As he moved, Zoya remained quiet. She'd long since learned to keep her mouth shut when she'd made her point. Eventually, the captain turned. 'If you come, you stay by my side and don't move an inch. Is that clear?'

'Yes.'

'And you do exactly what I tell you.'

Zoya nodded.

'In which case,' said Vaspine, 'you've got ten minutes to get ready. Move!'

19

A dozen thieves in total lined up on the deck, ready to go on the raid. They were all dressed in black, with tinted faces and blackened hair. A few exchanged glances when they spotted Zoya, but Zoya just smiled in return. To her left, Rosie sharpened her sabre sword as she chatted with another thief. Beebee was there too, strapping his wrists as if he was about to fight. To Beebee's right stood Cid, and addressing them all from the front was Vaspine.

Zoya saw Bucker leaning over the gunwale, paying no attention to the captain. She tiptoed behind him and tapped his shoulder. Bucker spun around, mouth already loaded with an excuse for why he hadn't been listening, when he saw Zoya and relaxed. 'Don't *do* that!' he said. 'I thought you were Mum!'

Zoya looked at Rosie, who was listening to the captain. 'Um, thanks!'

Bucker laughed. 'You're coming then?'

'If I stay close to him.'

Bucker leaned in. 'Don't worry, he said that to me on my first robbery. He soon forgets if he thinks you won't get yourself killed.'

Zoya climbed onto the gunwale.

'Can you see the ship?' asked Bucker. 'We've been tailing it for a while.'

In the distance was the silhouette of a large airship. Even from afar, it was almost big enough to eclipse the moon, creating a strange, ship-shaped corona that was both beautiful and creepy. Dotted along the cruiser's hull were the same faint lights Zoya had seen from the captain's cabin, except now she could see they were portholes. Accompanying these were new colourful flashes above the ship that flared and faded——spiderwebs, fountains, and wheels.

'Wow,' whispered Zoya. 'I thought you weren't allowed fireworks on airships.'

'You're not,' said Bucker, 'they startle other pilots. But the cruisers explode them anyway. It's amazing what you can get away with when you're rich.'

Zoya looked again at the cruiser and frowned. 'What's the plan, anyway?'

'There's a special dinner on the ship tonight, for the wealthy families who run the arms trade in this part of the sky' said Bucker. 'That's why there's fireworks. We're going to sneak on board, work our way up through the holds and meet at the dining hall. They won't know what's hit them.'

Zoya nodded. She started to drum her fingers on the lip of the gunwale.

Bucker glanced across. 'Are you scared?'

'About the raid?' Zoya stopped tapping. 'I guess. A bit. Though I reckon I'll be in no more danger there than I am here.'

Zoya realized her mistake immediately, but it was too late. Bucker's face lit up like a lantern when he understood what she'd said. A secret! Zoya figured she had about five seconds to think of an explanation and frantically racked her brain. But before Bucker could speak, Zoya was saved by Rosie, who leaned over and tugged at her sleeve. 'Zoya, you asked us to let you come along, so listen!'

Rosie turned back to the captain. Zoya glanced at Bucker, then smiled and shrugged. Before he could grab her, she slipped away and started to burrow through the crowd towards the front. By the time she arrived, the captain was just finishing his speech. His last words brought a cheer from the gathered thieves. Vaspine waited for it to fade, then turned to Cid, still smoking his pipe against the gunwale. 'Cid?'

'Boss?'

'Take us in.'

20

Over the course of the next hour, Cid steered the *Dragonfly* towards the cruiser. When they were within sight of its lookouts, Vaspine ordered all remaining lights on board to be extinguished. The airship was to proceed in total silence, its sleek shape invisible in the night sky. Zoya leaned her head over the side and listened to the wind skim the hull. The moon, now completely obscured, cast a faint glow over the cruiser's deck. When Zoya looked closely, she could just about make out the outlines of people.

She felt a tap on her shoulder. 'Let's go,' whispered Beebee.

It was difficult in the dark to work out where Beebee was leading her, so Zoya held onto the back of his T-shirt and hoped for the best. After a period of silent shuffling, they arrived at the ship's bow. Vaspine led the group through the clutter towards two small, open-topped crafts strapped to the deck. He stopped when he reached the first, then assigned each thief to one as they filed past.

'You're with me,' he said when it was Zoya's turn.

Zoya climbed into the nearest airship and sat beside Bucker. 'What now?' she whispered. Behind her, Vaspine assigned the final thief and leapt into the remaining seat.

'Now's the hard part,' said Bucker. 'We need to get onto their ship without them knowing.'

With a flick of the wrist, Vaspine gestured for both transporters to pull away. Their air motors whirred to life — then the crafts drifted in the direction of the cruiser. The thieves sat silent, gazing ahead or staring back at the *Dragonfly*, taking a rare opportunity to see the ship from below. The engines were so quiet Zoya felt uncomfortable, and she prayed for something to break the silence. She imagined a cough tickling someone's chest, and sure enough felt one in her own, scratching her throat. She slapped a hand to her mouth, ready to muffle the sound, but before she could cover it entirely the cough exploded in a short, sharp clap.

'Absolute silence,' said Vaspine, glaring at Zoya.

The transporters were gradually manoeuvring into a central position beneath the cruiser. Over the course of another minute, they glided closer until Zoya could hear the cruiser's keel creaking in the wind. They were so close that Vaspine was able to stand in his seat and knock softly on the bottom of the hull. He did this every so often, until he found the spot he was looking for and brought both transporters to a stop.

'Here,' he motioned to Beebee.

Beebee rose in his seat and pulled out of his footwell a contraption Zoya had never seen before. The size of his forearm, it had a polished handle and trigger at one end, and a serrated, circular blade at the other. Beebee hoisted the tool above his head, flicked a switch and started to cut into the hull. The device was almost silent.

'The Doc,' murmured Bucker.

'What?' whispered Zoya.

'The saw, it's the Doc's. He made it before he left. Works by vibration.'

Zoya watched Beebee cut a large circle into the cruiser's keel. The opening was wide enough to accommodate three men, and it took as many to hold the panel in place as Beebee started to round out the circle. After a few more seconds, he completed the job and the men manoeuvred the wooden plate down before tossing it over the side of the transporter. Zoya watched it disappear into the darkness.

'Everybody ready?' asked Vaspine.

The captain received a dozen whispered 'yes's. One by one, the thieves left their transporters and pulled themselves through the opening and onto the cruiser. The last on board was the captain, who pulled himself through and then nodded at the woman below whose job it was to fly the crafts back to the *Dragonfly*. Zoya watched her lash the vehicles together with a length of rope, then power the engines. As their only means of escape floated away, she felt a queasy sensation in her stomach. *We'd better get this right.*

Vaspine, on the other hand, seemed as calm as ever. In the dark of the hold, he flicked a match on his thumbnail and turned to address the raiders. 'Everyone into groups. Meet up in ten minutes. No mistakes and absolutely no casualties. Clear?'

'Clear.'

Vaspine blew out the light. 'Then let's go.'

21

Zoya stayed close to Vaspine as the other thieves fanned out in different directions. From the little she could see, they'd cut into the cruiser's engine bay. She was surrounded by large metal towers that stretched to the ceiling, each hissing and cracking rhythmically. The air in the room was hot and steamy, and there was an oil smell that made Zoya gag.

Vaspine led her through the maze—zigzagging left and right as if he'd done it a thousand times. After a while, Zoya realized they were heading for a patch of light at the far end of the deck. Standing in a doorway there, munching on a sandwich, was one of the cruiser's engineers.

'How are we going to get past?' whispered Zoya.

Vaspine, hiding behind an engine pump, winked. 'Watch.'

Keeping his head low, the captain scudded along the pump until he was just behind the engineer. The mechanic, oblivious, continued to chomp on his sandwich and stare into the distance. From his satchel, Vaspine pulled a short scrap of metal. He kissed it once, then dropped it into the gears that lined the pump's casing. The metal clattered between the gears, which eventually ground to a halt, wisps of smoke curling up from their sides. The engineer heard the noise, dropped his sandwich onto a nearby table and trudged over. Quicker than lightning, Vaspine leapt out from behind his hiding place, gripped the engineer at a point between his neck and shoulder, held him for a moment and then caught him as he sank to the floor.

Zoya shook her head, unable to believe what she'd just seen. One minute the man had been awake, then Vaspine had grabbed him and he was out. Before she could consider it any further, Vaspine summoned her. 'Help me lift him into that store room.'

Zoya grabbed the man's legs and lifted. The engineer was heavy, but together they managed to move him into the room. Once he was concealed, Vaspine dragged a couple of crates from a stack on the opposite wall and piled them in front of the door. This done, he took a handkerchief from his waistcoat and used it to dust his hands. 'The Odessan Grip,' he explained as he wiped. 'Knocks out a man quicker than a blow to the head.'

'How?' asked Zoya.

Vaspine grinned. 'Like this.'

He placed the thumb and forefinger of his right hand on Zoya's neck at exactly the spot he had on the engineer's. With only the smallest application of pressure, Zoya felt her pulse start to quicken, her vision to blur and pins and needles to prickle all over her body. Vaspine released the grip before Zoya followed the engineer to the floor. A few moments later, her senses returned to normal.

'Amazing.'

'Good,' said the captain, 'because you're doing the next one.'

Zoya's face dropped. Before she could protest, Vaspine had slipped through the door and started to make his way up the staircase into the belly of the ship. Zoya jogged to keep up, rubbing her neck where Vaspine had gripped it. Ahead, the captain moved like a cat, pouncing from wall to wall to avoid detection. Together, they slipped silently through the cruiser—past lounges, kitchens, bedrooms—sneaking when they could, knocking out anyone who got in their way. 'The last thing we need is them knowing we're here before we've properly arrived,' said Vaspine.

Eventually, they rounded a corner and came upon a set of oak double doors. Cut into a plaque above the doors were the words 'Dining Hall'. Beneath the plaque stood a food trolley, loaded with silver serving platters. Vaspine approached the trolley, picked up one of the trays and angled it so he could see his face, then proceeded to arrange his hair. Satisfied, he flashed a smile at Zoya, before thrusting open the doors. Inside, a hundred or so wealthy people looked up from their dinners. 'Stick 'em up, ladies and gentlemen,' said Vaspine, 'this is a raid!'

22

Slowly, the room silenced. The diners set down their cutlery and looked up at Vaspine and the other raiders, who'd burst in from different points around the room. Half their faces exhibited shock, the other half were alive with smiles. One or two even laughed.

'It's always like this,' whispered Bucker, who'd worked his way to Zoya from his entrance-point near the kitchen. 'Half realize it's a robbery and the other half think we're entertainment.'

As if to prove his point, a plump man with bushy sideburns stood up in his seat and started to clap. 'Bravo!' he said. 'This cruise just keeps getting better!'

The man's comment convinced more of the diners that the robbery was a performance, and they too cheered. They shouted even louder when a pair of Aviation Army soldiers standing guard started to move towards the intruders.

'Bop them on the nose for me,' said the man with the sideburns, faking a jab.

The soldiers looked like those Zoya had seen outside

the orphanage, the only difference being these had tasers in their hands.

Vaspine spotted the men stalking towards him and scanned the room for Beebee. He found him standing guard next to a dining table. Without a word, the captain communicated what he wanted the big man to do. Beebee, as if he were strolling along a sunny beach, stepped between the captain and the officers. Despite their considerable size, the men were dwarfed by Beebee, who stood a head taller than both. When they saw him, they pulled up. 'You can try those on me,' said Beebee, nodding at the tasers, 'but I'll feel no more than a tickle. You, on the other hand, when I catch you, will feel like a mountain's fallen.'

The soldiers stared at Beebee. Everyone in the dining hall held their breath. A few more seconds passed, during which the officers exchanged glances, then they made the silent decision to drop their tasers and slink back to the side of the room.

'Sorry to say this isn't a performance,' said Vaspine. 'I am the sky thief Carlos Vaspine and this is my crew. We're here to rob you. We're not here to hurt you. In a moment, these wonderful people are going to tie you to your chair with a length of rope. After we're gone, the rope is yours to keep. Think of it as a memento. In the meantime, you're all going to behave yourselves, else you'll be having a word with my friend here.' Vaspine turned to Beebee, who smiled.

For the next fifteen minutes, the raiders, including Zoya,

criss-crossed the hall, tying diners to their chairs and relieving them of their money and jewellery. Vaspine followed, talking to each passenger and assuring them their money was going to a good cause. 'Every single coin will end up in the hands of someone who needs it more than you or I,' he said to one irate lady. 'I hope that makes you feel a little better.'

Once everyone was secure and their valuables removed (Zoya had never seen so many coins, rings, necklaces, and bracelets in her life), Vaspine ordered his men to deposit their goodies in two sacks at the front of the hall. Rosie stood guard next to these, her sabre glinting in the light of the chandeliers. When they'd finished, the thieves made their way back to her side as Vaspine stepped forward. 'Thank you so much,' he said to the diners, 'you've all been wonderful. I'll be sure to rob you again.'

He waited for laughter. None came.

'Just my little joke,' he mumbled. 'Out of interest, which of you is the captain?'

Heads turned. Near the back of the room, a stocky man flicked strands of hair from his eyes and set his shoulders straight. 'I'm the captain. What do you want?'

'A word please, Mr . . . ?'

'Beefheart.'

'A word, Captain Beefheart.'

Beebee threaded his way through the tables, untied the captain from his chair and lifted him to his feet. Zoya used the distraction to sneak from Vaspine's side towards Bucker, who was absent-mindedly picking strawberries from the buffet. 'This is fun,' she whispered.

'I know!' said Bucker, popping another berry in his mouth.

'Not the strawberries, the raid!'

'Oh.' He smiled. 'Absolutely.'

Zoya noted his lack of enthusiasm. 'You don't think?'

'It's not that, it's just I've done it many times.' He shrugged. 'Listen, turn around. You'll like this bit.'

Zoya spun around to catch the cruiser's captain approaching Vaspine. Vaspine gripped the captain's shoulder roughly when he arrived and manoeuvred him so both their backs were to the diners. Beebee stood between the pair and the crowd, obscuring their view.

'What?' said Zoya.

Bucker nodded for her to continue watching.

After checking his concealment, Vaspine retracted his arm from the captain's and brushed the man's jacket. He pulled a pouch from his waistcoat and emptied its contents into the captain's hand. Five coins tumbled out, which he counted deliberately, before returning them to the pouch and slipping them inside the captain's pocket.

'Oh,' said Zoya, the truth dawning, 'he's in on it!'

Bucker laughed. 'Zoya, I like you, but you really are the slowest human being I've ever met.' And with that, he shuffled further down the buffet and started on the cakes.

23

One person most definitely not eating cake was the large man with the bushy sideburns who'd shouted 'Bravo!' when the thieves first burst into the hall. His initial excitement had morphed to fury now, and he glared at Vaspine and the cruiser captain, causing Zoya to do the same.

'This is brilliant,' said Vaspine. 'I owe you.'

'You owe me a hundred,' said the captain, being careful to keep his voice down. 'The Aviation Army has been round asking questions about all the airships that just *happen* to get robbed when I'm at the helm.'

Vaspine plucked another coin from his pocket and dropped it into Captain Beefheart's.

'It's going to take more than that this time, Carlos. They're really onto us. It wouldn't surprise me if they're watching now.'

Vaspine waved away the captain's worries.

'Either way,' continued Beefheart, 'we won't be able to do this again for a while. I want to give the Aviation Army someone else to chase.'

'That's fair,' said Vaspine, although he said it in a way that suggested he'd forget the moment he left the ship. 'Now, we'd better get you back to your seat. Usual plan?'

'The usual,' agreed Beefheart.

With that, the captain barged past Vaspine and Beebee towards the diners. Vaspine yelled after him in an exaggerated tone of offence. 'How dare you call us bandits? We're heroes!'

'You're bandits!' thundered Beefheart.

'Heroes!'

The captain turned around halfway back to his seat. 'Sir, true heroes have honour. They don't board defenceless ships, they don't rob passengers for all they're worth and they don't tie all the women to chairs like criminals.' He swept his hand around the room. 'A disgrace!'

'Now, hang on,' said Vaspine, storming in the captain's direction, before Beebee caught him and held him back.

'Yes, that's right, hold him,' exclaimed Beefheart. 'I'd rather avoid thumping him into next week if I can.' He threw up his hands in a gesture designed to excite the diners, who cheered him on.

'As if!' roared Vaspine. He shook his fist and strained to break free of Beebee.

And on it went.

Zoya followed the pantomime, until her attention was stolen by a movement in the corner of her eye. To her right, sat the man with the bushy sideburns. Like all passengers, he was bound to his chair, hands tied behind his back. Zoya couldn't put her finger on it, but there was something wrong about the way he was twisting and squirming. Before she could say anything, the man brought his arms out from behind his back and deposited a length of rope on the table. It took a moment for Zoya to recognize what was wrong about this, by which point the man had grabbed a steak knife and was bounding towards the front where Vaspine and Beefheart were continuing their performance.

Zoya stood paralyzed.

She waited for someone else to notice what was happening, but their attention was focused on the front. Time seemed to slow. The man bounded across the floor towards Vaspine, each step booming in Zoya's mind. She saw him raise the knife, ready to strike. A film of sweat formed on her forehead. Without thinking, Zoya started to move. She burst across the wooden floor, step by step, trying to catch him. Beebee heard her footsteps and turned to see what was happening. His entire body tensed when he saw the man, but he was too far away to help. Zoya doubled her speed until she was right behind him, then leapt onto his back. She clamped a forearm around the man's throat and yanked hard, so that he lost his footing and collapsed on top of her. Pinned, Zoya could hardly breathe. The man realized this, and a smirk spread across his face. He raised the steak knife . . .

Zoya screamed.

As she did, she thrust up her right hand, locking her thumb and finger around the man's neck. With only the smallest pressure, she felt his pulse start to quicken, then she watched his eyes glaze over as a small shudder ran through his body. After a moment, his eyelids closed and he started to slump. Zoya spotted the knife heading towards her chest and bucked the man with her knees, throwing him left as she rolled right. He hit the floor with a *thud*.

Without missing a beat, Vaspine jumped forwards. 'See, Beefheart, even your best man can't catch me.'

Beefheart understood Vaspine's trick and stifled a laugh.

'Yes, I'd laugh too if my airship was this easy to rob,' continued Vaspine, striding around the hall like it was a stage. He skipped to the window and glanced outside. Flying alongside the cruiser was the *Dragonfly*. 'Well, I can't stay around here all day,' he said, addressing the crowd, 'so if you'll excuse me, I need to fly.' With that, Vaspine rammed the butt of his dagger through the glass, stepped up to the frame and let himself fall.

The crowd gasped. Moments later, the remaining thieves started to follow. Zoya felt a hand grab her by the collar and drag her towards the window. The last thing she saw, as she was yanked backwards off the ship, was the bewildered face of the passenger with the sideburns who was just waking up.

24

After everything that had happened, the escape from the cruiser proved to be relatively uneventful. Vaspine caught everyone as they landed back on the *Dragonfly*. After checking they were OK and ensuring they'd left no one behind, he nodded at Cid to get them out of there. Cid did so leisurely, aware the behemoth cruiser couldn't manoeuvre quickly enough to follow.

The thieves that had taken part in the raid went their separate ways, busy with one job or another. Bucker had to work a night-shift, so he knuckled Zoya on the top of the arm to say goodbye, then scurried up the mainmast.

Zoya's heart still pounded from the excitement, and she decided to stay out on deck for a while to calm down before going to bed. Everything she'd read about sky thieves—the swashbuckling, the gold and jewels, the daring escapes—was nothing compared to the real thing. The break-in, stalking through the cruiser, Vaspine tricking the crowd, Beefheart, her tussle with the fat man, the captain's theatrical exit—all of it set Zoya's mind alight. She wanted to be a sky thief, there was no doubt about that now.

She'd have to work. Kane might care about her heritage, but it would mean little to the crew of the *Dragonfly*. The ship was a well-oiled machine. Every cog had its job. Zoya needed to find a gap, something only she could do, something to make the machine run even more smoothly. *Saving the captain's life was a good start.*

The deck remained quiet while Zoya was outside, apart from one moment of panic when Bucker spotted an airship tailing them off the starboard side. Some of the crew talked themselves into thinking it was an Aviation Army patrol ship on its way to round them up, but Cid shooed away such thoughts. 'If that's a patrol ship,' he said, 'then I'm a magician's apprentice.'

Cid's confidence did little to comfort those on deck, who waited anxiously until the unidentified ship flew close enough to be identified as a commercial freighter. 'Abracadabra,' said Cid.

Zoya went to bed, leaving the pilot cackling on the bridge.

The sun was already high when she was woken by a member of the crew and ordered to the captain's quarters. Zoya arrived to find Vaspine counting the goodies they'd stolen the previous evening. 'It's tough being a sky thief,' he said, not looking up, 'constantly on the run, trying to beat other ships to the treasure. But a haul like this makes it all worthwhile.'

'Definitely,' agreed Zoya. 'I could live off that for the rest of my life.'

'You could,' said Vaspine, 'but you won't. Every penny of this will go to people who need it.' He paused and stared at Zoya, then tossed her a cloth and a grubby coin. 'Clean this,' he said. Zoya picked up the cloth and started to rub. 'That was a smart thing you did last night, saving my life. Perhaps you'll be more useful than I thought.'

Zoya nodded. 'I loved it. It's the most exciting thing I've ever done.'

'If I had one of these for every time a young thief said that . . .' Vaspine examined a coin under the lamplight.

'So robberies aren't always good?'

'Oh, they're always fun,' said Vaspine. 'It's the rest that isn't as exciting.'

'How do you mean?' asked Zoya, scraping away at a stubborn speck of grime.

The captain lowered his coin and padded to the window. He pulled back the blinds, revealing a view of the deck, then gestured to the thieves—some chatting, some waiting, some rushing around, some fixing the ship, some cleaning. 'That's the average life of a sky thief,' said Vaspine. 'It's not the most glamorous.'

'But there are robberies, right?'

'Yes,' said Vaspine, drawing the curtains and returning to his desk, 'but keeping the ship up and running—especially one as old as this—takes up most of our time.'

'I'll help,' said Zoya.

Vaspine nodded. 'The crew'll like that. See, I promised your parents I'd keep you and that locket away from Kane, but the rest of them aren't so foolish. They don't have a clue yet who's after them. If you want them to protect you when the time comes, you're going to have to become one of them. And that means working like them. Let me see that coin.'

Zoya tossed the coin over. It gleamed under the lantern. 'Have we heard any more?' she asked.

'About Kane?'

Zoya nodded.

'Nothing.'

Zoya bit her lip. 'What are we going to do?'

Vaspine manipulated Zoya's coin through his fingers. After a moment, he rapped it on the desk. 'I'm working on it,' he said. 'For now, just be vigilant. If you see anything out of the ordinary, come tell me. And Zoya?'

'Yes.'

'Don't worry.'

With that, Vaspine nodded at his door and gestured for Zoya to leave. She closed the door behind her and stood on the deck. If there was one lesson she'd learned it was that the time someone tells you not to worry is precisely the time you should start worrying.

25

Zoya spent the entire morning after her meeting with the captain performing so many acts of sweeping, wiping, scraping, mopping, and dusting that, by the time she ran into Bucker stumbling across the deck, an hour late for his next lookout shift, she was more than happy to accept his offer of a break.

'Besides,' said Bucker, glancing at the welts already forming on Zoya's hands, 'that really doesn't look like fun.'

Bucker led them up the mainmast and into his pod, where he threw himself onto a pile of cushions and groaned. He proceeded to arrange the space, placing each object where he liked it. When he was finished, he sat back and stared at Zoya. After a few seconds, he leaned forward and raised a finger as if he was about to speak, then sat back again and continued to stare. Zoya looked at him like he'd gone mad. Eventually, he spoke. 'My mum told me not to ask you what I'm about to ask you, but I think you want to tell me so I'm going to ask anyway.'

'OK . . .' said Zoya.

94

'Last night, when we were watching the fireworks before the cruiser raid, you said something about being in danger. What did you mean?'

The blood rushed to Zoya's cheeks. 'I didn't.'

'Zoya, if you lie to me again I'm going to push you out of this pod. Then you will be in danger.'

There was a spark in Bucker's eye that told Zoya he meant it. 'If I tell you,' she said, 'you can't tell anyone. Promise?'

'Promise.'

Zoya proceeded to tell Bucker her whole story—her time at the orphanage, the day she went to the museum, her encounter with Kane, Mr Whycherley, the kidnap, her attempted escape, everything Vaspine had told her about her mother and father and the locket—everything.

At the end of her tale, Bucker backed up against the side of the lookout pod and let out a rush of air. 'Wow,' he said. 'I was expecting something cool, but nothing like that. Ha! You're Jupiter's daughter. You're famous!'

Zoya blushed.

'Can I have a look?'

Zoya reached for her locket. Vaspine had warned her to keep it hidden, but there was something about the way Bucker had asked that made her want to trust him. No, there was something about *Bucker* that made her want to trust him. She unclipped the pendant from around her neck and placed it in his hand.

'It's heavy,' he said.

The locket was the shade of onyx, its chain formed of black and blue beads the size of lentils and its pendant oval-shaped and smooth like a pebble. Bucker juggled it in his hands to get a sense of its weight, then let it rest in his palm. 'So, what is it he wants?'

'Kane?'

Bucker nodded.

'I don't know,' said Zoya. 'I wish I did.'

Zoya let Bucker hold the locket for a few more seconds, then lifted it out of his hands and refastened it around her neck. For a while, they sat in silence. The airship flew through a busy sky, and Zoya could see half a dozen ships around them, weaving in and out of each other as if dancing. In the distance, hazy in the shade of a mountain, she spied one ship larger than all the others combined—a linked hexagon of grey and orange platforms, some of which housed tall white buildings, and others cranes and ladders and walkways. Above it was a projected image, although what it was Zoya struggled to make out.

'What's that?' she asked Bucker.

Bucker glanced over his shoulder. 'Oh, it's an Aviation Army airbase.' He looked off the starboard side. The ship was drifting in the opposite direction. 'Good, Cid's seen it.'

'No,' said Zoya. 'I mean the projection.'

'Ah, all the airbases have one. It's like a hologram map of

the region, marks any thunderheads, tornadoes, hurricanes, dust-storms.' He squinted in the morning light. 'Why? Don't tell me there's a tornado coming.'

Zoya chuckled. But something about the screen troubled her. She leaned back in Bucker's pod and grabbed a spyglass from beneath a pile of cushions. With the glass in place, she could see the base clearly. She ran her eye over the scene, looping up and down the cranes, and closing in on individual soldiers, amused she could see them when they didn't even know she existed. Eventually, she trained the glass on the image. When she did, a small noise escaped her mouth.

'What's up?' asked Bucker

Zoya didn't respond. Projecting fifty feet tall and as wide as a house, standing with his top hat and cane, was a perfect representation of Lendon Kane.

26

Zoya peered at the hologram. Its edges were fuzzy, but it was definitely Kane—the eyes, the moustache, the wiry body—they all belonged to the man in black. With the spyglass still to her eye, she reached back, gripped Bucker's shirt and tugged him over. 'I don't think that's showing the weather.'

Bucker looked again at the airbase. This time, he too spotted the odd shape where the map should have been, and snatched the glass from Zoya. For a few seconds, he regarded the hologram. He opened his mouth to speak, but before he could say anything they heard a commotion down on the deck. They went to investigate.

Bucker and Zoya joined a small crowd that had formed outside Vaspine's quarters. From her position at its edge, Zoya could see Rosie, Beebee, and Cid marshalling the others and ordering them away from the airbase.

'What's going on?' Bucker asked a nearby crew member.

'There's something wrong with the weather map.'

Cid spotted Bucker. He shot out a hand and dragged the

younger boy from the crowd. 'How long's it been like that?' he asked, nodding at the hologram.

'I don't know,' said Bucker. 'We just saw it.'

A moment later, the door to Vaspine's quarters swung open and the captain strode out. He whistled once to get the attention of the crowd. 'Ladies and gentlemen, nice though a bit of excitement is, we've all seen a malfunctioning weather screen before and I'm sure we'll see one again. Right now, I need you to get back to work.'

The crowd groaned.

'I know,' said the captain. 'All the same, back to your posts. Last one there is on half rations.'

Zoya rocked on her heels, unsure if Vaspine's order also applied to her and Bucker. The captain caught this and held out a hand. 'Not you two,' he said. 'Stand with me.'

They waited for the last of the thieves to leave, then scampered over to the captain. A shadow ghosted across the *Dragonfly*'s deck as an airship passed above. Clouds of black smoke from the craft's oil engine drifted down as a second airship cut across their bow. Passengers leaned over its side, their eyes fixed on the hologram.

Vaspine called over his shoulder. 'Cid, take us to the base.'

The pilot glanced at Rosie and Beebee, then back at the captain. 'Boss, we don't want to get any closer to an Aviation Army airbase.'

'Cid,' said Vaspine, sharply. 'Take us in.'

The pilot shook his head, then trudged off towards the bridge.

'Is . . .' Rosie paused, deciding whether to ask the question. 'Is that thing wearing a top hat?'

Vaspine nodded.

'So it's Kane?'

'What the hell's he up to this time?' said Beebee.

The captain glanced briefly at Zoya, then back at the airbase. Over the course of the next few minutes, Cid swung the *Dragonfly* around so it was aimed at the floating fortress, then buzzed the engine. A crowd of nearby airships did the same, until they formed a procession — all lined up neatly — freighters, airbuses, and an Aviation Army patrol ship trying to get back to base. Ahead of the *Dragonfly*, yet more ships started to bunch around the hologram.

Zoya heard a noise, growing louder as they drew closer. It seemed to emanate from somewhere near the image, amplified so it echoed across the sky. Zoya shared a glance with Bucker, then cupped a hand to her ear. She listened, but the sound was too muddy to make out.

Eventually, the *Dragonfly* approached the crowd of airships. Cid manoeuvred the craft so that it nestled behind an airbus, then resumed his position with the others. 'I really don't think this is a good idea, cap',' he said. Climbing over the projection's base now was a handful of Aviation Army soldiers, trying to work out what had gone wrong. Vaspine ignored Cid and turned his attention to the airbus. He searched for the ship's captain and spotted him not far off, studying the hologram. 'I say,' he called, adopting a friendly tone, 'what's going on?'

The airbus captain—a short man in a peaked cap—peeled his eyes from the airbase and approached Vaspine. 'Damned mystery,' he said. 'Apparently, all the maps in the region are doing it.' He looked at the Aviation Army soldiers and rolled his eyes. 'Poor sods seem utterly bamboozled.'

Zoya looked again at the hologram. One of the soldiers had made his way to the centre of the platform now and was fighting to keep his footing beside the tip of Kane's cane. Visible through the mist was a brass projection chamber as tall as the soldier, spinning above which were two metal wheels. The soldier retrieved a hammer from his belt and swung at the lowest. The iron *clanked* as it connected with the wheel, and for a moment the sound Zoya had heard earlier stopped. The soldier beamed and raised his hands in victory. But no sooner had he done this than the noise restarted, louder than before. This time, Zoya recognized the rumble as a man's voice. Captain Vaspine noticed this too, and he held up a hand to silence everyone behind him.

27

'. . . when I was seventeen, I killed a man for stealing my share of a robbery. I laughed when he pleaded for his life. When I was twenty, I threw a man off my airship for sending me the wrong way out of an airgate.'

Kane's voice boomed out, clear now. His head rolled from side to side as he spoke, his eyes distant. The recorded hologram—a mix of sepia and blue—flickered ahead of the airbase, distorting whenever a strong gust of wind blew across the valley.

'When I was twenty-four, I murdered an old man who tried to betray me to the Aviation Army. Aged thirty, I killed three of my crew who demanded I pay them more for their services.'

Kane blinked slowly, then stared at the airships gathered ahead. He held their gaze for a long time, his eyes darkening, then he spoke. 'My point, of course, is that I react poorly when anyone tries to stop me achieving my goal. You and I have known each other a long time, Carlos. You could have joined me after the mutiny.' Kane paused, and extended a hand, its palm up. 'But you chose a different path.'

Back on the *Dragonfly*, Captain Vaspine leaned against the gunwale, his arms stretched out at the side, gripping the wood. Zoya could see his knuckles were white. A few feet away, Rosie, Cid, and Beebee stared at the hologram, their faces dark. 'What's going on?' asked Beebee.

'Quiet!' snapped the captain.

'Jupiter's locket is mine,' continued Kane, his voice vibrating the deck beneath Zoya's feet. 'As is the crystal in his vault. You managed to hide the girl from me for ten years. But no more.'

Zoya shuddered. Her hand shot to her locket. She felt the hologram's eyes bore into her like a snake's, so hot and powerful she had to look away. The airships surrounding the *Dragonfly* had silenced now, so that the only sounds in the valley were those of creaking decks and rippling sails. Somewhere off on a ship to her left, she heard a child cry.

'The *Dragonfly* is no match for the *Shadow*,' continued Kane. 'Right now, I do not know where you are, but let me tell you,' Kane's hologram leaned forward, looming over the gathered airships and obscuring the airbase, 'and it's something I want you to remember, the first thing you think of when you wake and the last thing before you go to sleep. Remember it good, because you can bet your life on it.' Kane's face twisted to a mask of fury, his teeth bared, his eyes white. 'I am coming.'

The hologram disappeared.

Where Kane's figure had towered was now just the old airbase, glinting in the sun. The airships nearby remained silent for a few seconds, punctuated every now and then by a cough. Then whispers started to fly. From the airbus next door, Zoya heard the captain turn to one of his passengers. 'They've found Jupiter's locket?' He raised an eyebrow. 'I would *not* want to be on the *Dragonfly* right now.'

Zoya looked at Captain Vaspine. Cid, Rosie, and Beebee remained motionless, their shoulders rocks. The captain met each of their gazes in turn, then let his eyes linger on Zoya. 'Meeting,' he said to them all through gritted teeth. 'My quarters. Now.'

28

Vaspine nearly tore the door off its hinges as he entered his cabin. Behind him filed Rosie, Cid, Beebee, Zoya, and Bucker. Each took a seat, then fixed their eyes on the captain. Vaspine stalked the room, unhooking his weapon belt from his waist and flinging it to the floor. 'How the hell did he do that?' he growled.

The others centred their gazes on Cid. 'Simple enough,' said the pilot. 'You just get a man on the inside and wait until no one's looking.'

'It's an Aviation Army airbase!' said Vaspine.

Cid shrugged.

'And why haven't we seen it before now?' snapped Vaspine. 'That airbus captain said every map in the region's like this. The lookout should have seen them.'

Cid glanced at Bucker, then away again before Vaspine could catch it. 'They saw nothing,' he said.

'Carlos, this isn't the lookout's fault,' said Rosie. 'It's ours. And yours. How can you expect us to be prepared for this kind of thing when you don't even tell us what's happening?'

Vaspine sighed. 'That's fair.'

Rosie glanced at Zoya. 'Was Kane telling the truth? Is Jupiter's locket real? Does she have it?'

Vaspine nodded.

'But how do you know for sure?'

Vaspine fixed her with a stare. 'I know.'

Rosie lifted herself off the arm of the sofa. She paced across the room, then back. 'Am I the only one who thinks there's something we're not being told?'

'What do you mean?' asked Beebee.

'Like, why does Kane happen to leave us this message two days after Zoya arrives? And where did she find Jupiter's locket?'

Beebee looked at the captain. 'Is she right?'

The captain walked to his desk and leaned on it with both hands. 'She's right.'

'Carlos,' said Rosie, 'sooner or later you're going to have to tell us the whole story. It might as well be now while we can still do something about it.'

Vaspine glanced at Zoya. 'Up to you, kid?'

Zoya looked at each of the adults in turn. 'OK.' She nodded. 'Tell them.'

Vaspine proceeded to tell Rosie, Cid, and Beebee the whole story—all about his time on the *White Knight*, the night of the mutiny, his smuggling Zoya to Richard Whycherley's orphanage, everything.

The room went silent. Vaspine crossed to the bookshelf. He brought down a red, leather-backed volume and rifled through its pages until he found what he was looking for. Inside, was a picture of Jupiter, Dominika, and Zoya's locket. Vaspine pointed to the locket on the page, then the identical one around Zoya's neck. Cid took the book, held it up to Zoya and laughed. 'I'll be damned,' he said.

As they studied the book, Vaspine moved across to the skymap. 'There's just one more thing,' he said. The captain leaned down and opened a panel on the cabinet. The 3D image inlaid in the map started to change, first blurring then focusing on a section in the upper-left corner. As the image resolved, Zoya started to make out a mass of rock. Her view was from above and slightly at an angle, but it was clear from its shadow that the rock was floating.

Vaspine spotted Zoya looking. 'The Island in the Sky,' he explained. 'The sky thieves' international home. A giant, floating island. No one knows how it works, but it's an entire world, with forests, mountains, and rivers. And some of the most dangerous pirates in the sky.'

He turned to Zoya. 'Your father kept a vault on the island.'

'Is that what this is all about?' said Rosie. 'Jupiter's vault? I thought that was a myth?'

'So do many,' said Vaspine. 'But it's true. Rumour's long had it filled with gold and jewels. But its real worth might lie beyond mere trinkets.' The captain tapped a button at the side of the map. The image changed, dissolving and reforming on a baked desert. Tall dunes banded the dull yellow, and in the centre was an oval, its rim raised an inch above the sand. 'The Desert of Tamertin.'

'I know this one,' said Zoya, scrunching her face as she tried to recall. 'It's the crystals.'

Vaspine nodded. 'The Algrond Crystals.'

Zoya had learned about the minerals in a library book. A crystal meteorite had fallen in the Tamertin desert, striking the ground and carving out the crater on Vaspine's map. So destructive was the force that it had shattered the crystal at its heart, hurling fragments hundreds of miles. In the end, four had been recovered, and subsequently analysed by boffins in Tamertin, who revealed them to be made of a substance never seen before. Each piece was worth the wealth of an entire empire.

'No one knows for sure whether the crystal's in your father's vault. If it is, he never showed me. But Kane's convinced. After I left, he ransacked the ship for the key. When he couldn't find it, he went to the vault and tried to break in. But Jupiter was a smart man. He made his vault of grapheus. That's the strongest stuff there is. To have broken through, Kane would have needed all the explosives on the planet.' Vaspine paused. 'Or that key around your neck.'

29

'This is the key?' Zoya clutched at her locket.

Vaspine nodded. 'Like I said, your father was smart.' Vaspine returned to his chair. 'And that brings us to now. Kane's message tells us he hasn't given up. He's craved that Algrond Crystal for a decade. He won't give up easily. Destroying our ship will mean nothing if it brings him the crystal.'

'Then we take him out,' said Beebee. 'Cid flies us in at night and we hit him with a surprise attack.'

'We'd be dead in minutes,' said Rosie.

'Seconds,' corrected Vaspine. 'His ship's vastly superior. We can't fight.'

Rosie gestured at Zoya. 'What about just giving him the locket? Be done with it?'

Zoya's hand shot to her chest. The thought of giving away her pendant filled her with dread. Not only was it her good-luck charm, it was now her only link to her parents. Zoya was just getting ready to say this when Vaspine shook his head. 'No. I made a promise ten years ago to get Zoya and the locket to safety.'

'But we can't hide,' said Beebee.

'We won't hide,' said Vaspine. 'But we might have to run.'

Cid rose from his chair. 'I don't like it. If there's one thing I've learned from all these years of flying it's that you can run in the skies for a while, but sooner or later you get caught. And everyone knows, Kane always gets his prey.'

'Not necessarily.' For a few seconds, the captain rummaged around his desk, then returned to the group with a hand-drawn map. He cleared the table near the sofa and laid the map face-up on the wood. It appeared to have been drawn by the captain, sketched in the same red ink he kept on his desk. In the middle was a doodle of an airship. Surrounding this were forests, rivers, and lakes, as well as villages and towns, including a large metropolis called Dalmacia. The captain allowed everyone a few seconds to familiarize themselves with the scene, then pointed to a series of mountains to the left of the airship. Zoya squinted to read its name: The Dalmacian Mountain Range. 'Look closer,' said Vaspine. 'Follow the Dalmacians.'

Zoya laid a finger at the southern-most point of the range and traced north, following the mountains until they reached the ocean. She moved along the chain once, then again, and was about to give up when she spotted another doodle. Inscribed into the mountains, just north of the *Dragonfly*, was a gap in the peaks. She read its name. 'The Dalmacia Pass.'

Cid thrust himself away from the table. 'Of course!'

'What?' asked Zoya.

'Our captain. He's a clever man.'

'What?' asked Bucker.

Vaspine plucked the map from beneath Rosie and Beebee's noses and deposited it back on his desk. 'The Dalmacia Pass is a narrow canyon that leads into the range. It's got an airgate at the end that runs through the mountains to the other side.'

'And?' said Bucker.

Vaspine inhaled. 'And Kane's *Shadow* is an enormous ship. So big, in fact, that if it tried to get through the gate it would bring down the mountain.'

Suddenly, Zoya understood. 'So we slip through and they can't follow.'

'Precisely.'

'But, what do we do after that?'

'We'll cross that bridge when we come to it.'

Rosie had been listening to the others without speaking. She shook her head, approached Vaspine's desk and retrieved the map. She studied it, then laid it down. 'One problem,' she said. 'What if Kane finds us before we get to the pass? The *Shadow*'s much faster. Even if we saw that black and red monstrosity a mile off, we couldn't outrun him.'

'Let's get the Doc,' interjected Cid. The others stared at him as if he'd suggested they eat their own feet. 'Seriously, if we pick him up, maybe he can speed us up? I'd like to see Kane catch me then!'

Vaspine shook his head. 'It'd take too long. Besides, he wouldn't come. No, we're on our own here.' He swiped a hand in front of him, ending the discussion. 'But that's something for me to worry about. In the meantime, I want the rest of you to go back to work. We need to be ready. Kane might appear at any time.'

Cid cleared his throat. 'OK, so where do I fly us?'

Vaspine opened his cabin door and nodded for them to leave. 'North,' he said, 'to the Dalmacians. It's time we put some distance between us and this top-hat-wearing psychopath.'

30

Vaspine tapped Zoya's shoulder as she passed. 'A moment.'

Zoya stepped aside. Vaspine waited for the last of the others to leave, then closed the door. He walked to his desk, pulled out a chair and motioned for Zoya to sit. 'Rosie wasn't lying,' he said. 'We certainly have the weaker airship. But we've faced worse odds and won.'

'Thanks,' said Zoya.

'Don't thank me yet. Promising to protect someone and actually doing it are two different things.' He made a steeple of his hands and stared at Zoya over the top. 'That's where you come in.'

'Me?'

'You didn't think we'd do everything, did you?'

'Well, no . . .'

'Good. You see, if Kane's chasing us then I need to know you can fight. If we can't get to the pass in time, or if Kane catches us before we make it, you need to be able to handle yourself.'

Zoya shook her head. 'He could be here any time. I can't learn to fight in a day.'

'No,' he said. 'But that doesn't mean you shouldn't start. Besides, you're lucky you're on the *Dragonfly*. If anyone can get you up to speed, it's Rosie.'

Zoya furrowed her brow. Sensing her confusion, Vaspine rolled his eyes and walked to the cabin door. He twisted the handle, then made a thumbing motion for Zoya to leave. She passed under his outstretched arm and into the morning sun. Before she was out of earshot, the captain called after her. 'Find Rosie. Tell her to give you the choice.'

'The choice?' muttered Zoya.

'You'll see.'

The ship was gliding through cloud-stuffed skies, so that a mist had engulfed the decks, streaming over the gunwale and giving everything a close, hazy appearance. Zoya trudged through the vapour, trying to get her head around what had happened. All the stories she'd read about Kane, all the nasty tales, were scary. But now that she'd seen his message—the chilling smile, the icy eyes, that deep commanding voice— his chasing her became real.

Zoya made a conscious effort to focus.

She expected to find Rosie out on deck, fencing with a group of thieves. But that afternoon there was no sign of her. Zoya visited every corner of the ship where Rosie might be hidden, but still nothing. She started to ask the crew whether they'd seen her, but they either answered negatively or gave Zoya directions, only for her to arrive and find nobody. It was only when Zoya grew hungry and went to grab some food that she eventually stumbled across a clue. The serving chef, a scrawny man with a fish earring and a tattoo of a ladle on his forearm, perked up at the mention of Rosie's name. 'Oh,' he said, dumping another potato onto Zoya's plate, 'she owes me a few coins. I bet she's down at the armoury.'

'Where's that?' asked Zoya, abandoning her plate on the counter.

The chef opened his mouth to explain, then thought better of it. Sighing, he leaned back into the kitchen. 'Maddie, can you cover for me? I need to take the new girl somewhere.'

From the kitchen, Zoya heard the clatter of pans. 'Charlie Barley, always asking me to . . .'

Charlie started to mimic his colleague's grumbles, before removing his apron and ducking under the counter. Zoya followed him out of the mess hall—much to the irritation of the other thieves, who looked despairingly between the vanishing chef and the empty food stand—and along the deck. Bulbous clouds had replaced the hazy ones now. Big, wet raindrops bounced off the deck and onto Zoya's clothes, soaking her. Charlie led her towards the bridge, which was empty apart from one of Cid's deputies. When he spotted Charlie, the deputy glanced up from his book. 'Good afternoon.'

'If this is a good afternoon,' said Charlie, 'I'd hate to see a bad one.'

Charlie led Zoya past the bridge to a section of the ship she'd yet to explore. This new area was similar to the bow, filled with the same junk. Charlie walked to a barrel wedged in a dim corner and dragged it aside. He revealed a square opening, just about wide enough to fit a person, that led down to a staircase. He unhooked a lantern from the gunwale and handed it to Zoya. 'The armoury's down there. I'd give you the exact directions, but they're complicated and you'll know when you get near, anyway.'

'How?'

'Ever heard the sound of a dozen swords being sharpened?'

Zoya shook her head.

'Well, you're about to.'

Zoya lowered the lantern into the opening. Its light illuminated a little way ahead, before fading to dark. She turned to the chef. 'What if I get lost?'

Charlie shrugged. 'Then you'll be in trouble.'

Zoya frowned, then thanked the cook and started to edge backwards into the belly of the ship. As she disappeared, the chef called after her. 'And tell Rosie to bring me my money!'

31

The lower decks of the *Dragonfly* reminded Zoya of the orphanage roof: dark, dank, and disgusting. Were it not for the lantern, she doubted she'd have seen anything, and Zoya made a silent prayer the flame would last. A series of icy water droplets hit her neck and ran down her back, making her jump. When she did, Zoya noticed for the first time her feet were wet. Angling the lantern towards the floor, it revealed a puddle of brown rainwater. *Great*.

With little choice, Zoya shook off her feet and plodded forward into the black, trying to pick out the metallic scrape of sharpening blades above all the other *clanks* and *squarks* of the airship. For the next few minutes, she stumbled through a labyrinth of corridors that almost made her dizzy. She poked her head into countless rooms and opened as many doors, only to find storage cupboards or bedrooms or toilets. All the while, she listened for the armoury. In time, she lost her bearings and started to search randomly, plunging the lantern ahead to avoid stumbling over a pile of crates or a sack of onions.

Eventually, Zoya noticed a smudge of light at the end of the corridor and started to move towards it. She no longer cared if it was the armoury, she just wanted air. The lit-up square grew in her vision, until she ducked beneath a crossbeam and realized, with a start, that she was outside. Zoya had emerged onto a viewing balcony that extended from the *Dragonfly*'s hull. Stretching away either side was the hull itself, curving backwards until it disappeared. It had stopped raining, although the clouds lingered. Zoya inhaled the damp air and lowered her lantern.

The balcony's balustrade was made from iron. Zoya rested her arms across it, shivering when her skin touched the cold metal. Not far below, a brace of curved highlights illuminated the top of a bank of clouds. Beyond, lay solid ground. Peering down, Zoya felt stupid. There she was, miles high, being pursued by the world's most vicious sky thief, tasked with learning how to fight, and she couldn't even find her teacher. 'Useless,' she muttered.

Zoya unclasped her locket and dangled it over the edge. She watched it dance in the breeze and felt an urge to let go. Doing so would solve everything. Kane would leave her alone, and the *Dragonfly* too. She could return to her old life on the surface, go back to the orphanage, see her friends. And yet, Zoya couldn't do it. She couldn't drop the locket. It meant too much to her. And now it was the key to her father's vault. The crystal, the gems, all that money—she couldn't let Kane get his hands on any of it.

'Must be tempting,' said a voice from behind.

Zoya bunched her hand around the locket and turned to see Rosie duck beneath the crossbeam.

'I wouldn't blame you,' continued Rosie. 'It's an awfully small thing to be causing such a big problem.'

Zoya shook her head. 'I can't.'

'I know,' said Rosie. 'So why are you dangling it off an airship?'

Zoya shrugged and brought her hands back behind the railing.

'So, that's Jupiter's key?' said Rosie. 'Do you know how it works?'

'No,' said Zoya. 'I didn't know it was a key until the captain told me.' Zoya stared at the clouds near the horizon.

'How are you feeling?' asked Rosie.

'Not great.'

A moment's silence passed. Rosie pointed in the direction of a break in the clouds. 'Do you see that waterfall?'

Zoya looked down. Far below the airship was the summit of a large mountain. Tumbling off the side was a narrow, silvery waterfall. She nodded.

'Follow the water down a little ways.'

Zoya closed an eye and used her finger to trace the path of the stream, which carved a valley into the mountain before widening. She followed the river to the horizon, where the valley gave way to deep gorges that burrowed into harder rock. As it disappeared, Zoya noticed the river swell further, until it was almost as wide as the mountain from which it had flown.

'Big, huh?'

'Huge.'

'That enormous river from a tiny waterfall. Isn't it interesting how small things grow big in the end?' Rosie turned her back to the view. 'You know, I saw you trembling when you were listening to Kane's message. I don't blame you, it must have been pretty terrifying. But that's no excuse. When someone's after you, you can't show any weakness. You've got to be tough.'

'I am,' said Zoya.

'Yeah?'

'Yeah. In fact, the captain said I should ask you for the choice.'

Rosie paused. 'He did?'

'He says I need to learn how to fight.'

Rosie chuckled. She picked up Zoya's lantern and started to make her way back into the airship. 'Sorry, you're too young to learn anything useful in the time we've got.'

'I'm not!' said Zoya, following.

'I like my students to be able to at least hold a sword.'

'I can,' said Zoya. 'Let me try.'

Rosie halted. She stared at Zoya for a long time. Eventually, she spoke. 'OK.' She spread her palms in defeat. 'Let's see if you're as sharp as the captain's telling me.'

Zoya smiled. 'When do we start?'

Rosie lifted her watch and squinted at the time. 'Now.'

32

A globe of light illuminated the tunnel as Rosie slipped in and out of the shadows. Zoya did her best to follow, listening for the sound of the older woman's footsteps. 'Where are we going?' she called into the darkness.

'Patience.'

After a particularly troublesome series of bends, the light ahead of Zoya disappeared. Rosie's footsteps stopped too, forcing Zoya to jog to avoid losing her. She rounded a final corner and found Rosie standing in a cramped alcove. The lamp in her right hand cast a kaleidoscope of shapes onto her face. Behind her, Zoya spotted a doorway. Rosie raised her eyebrows, then led her into the centre of a gym. From her pocket, she fetched a box of matches, struck one and proceeded to light a couple of lanterns on the walls. Even when lit they barely provided enough light to see. The room's floor was covered by a stained and torn leather mat that squelched with every step. At the foot of each wall was a wooden bench, piled high with sweat-rags, masks, discarded gloves, blades, hilts, and training diagrams. In one corner was a heap of gym equipment—skipping ropes, climbing frames—and in another a collection of swords and daggers. Zoya reached out to touch one.

'Wait!' said Rosie, as she swung a scabbard around her waist.

Zoya froze. 'Why are we training in the dark?'

Rosie finished attaching the scabbard, walked to the swords, selected two and pulled them from their guards. As she made her way back to Zoya, she started to swing the swords around her head at a speed that made Zoya dizzy.

'Fighting in the light and dark are very different,' she said, continuing to whirl the blades. 'If you end up fighting with one of these, you're going to have to do it in sunshine, at night, when it's cloudy, rainy, snowy. If I only teach you how to fight in the light, you'll only be able to fight in the light. If I teach you in the dark, light is your advantage.'

Rosie allowed the swords to circumvent her head one more time, then let go. The blades arced through the air and landed next to each other, embedded into the wood. 'It's time to make your choice,' she said, retiring to the edge of the room. 'Everyone I train has to make this decision. This is going to be your sword so choose carefully.'

Zoya examined the two weapons. The left sword looked plain in comparison to the right. Its blade was a dull metal, with inscriptions close to the hilt. Zoya tried to read the words, but they were too scratched to decipher. The hilt was formed of a darker, bluish metal that swept away from the blade like a pair of bull's horns. The pommel at the end had a cross in the middle and two spikes angled perpendicular to the blade.

The second sword was a work of art in comparison. Its blade was unlike any Zoya had seen. Half appeared to have been sheared away, its edge serrated and razor-sharp. The other half curved from the serrated edge like a wave. This second blade was without a cross-guard, but its grip was flame orange and caught Zoya's eye like the sun.

Zoya wanted to choose the second weapon, but she sensed a test. Something about the first blade's plain looks made her think it would be the better choice. 'I'll have the one with the horns.'

Rosie grinned. 'Storm.' She pulled the fiery orange blade from the ground and tossed it onto a pile in the corner. 'You chose well. That pretty sword would have got you killed before you got it out of its sheath. And that, Zoya, is your first lesson: the best sword is always the strongest. Storm's a beauty. Now, come here.'

Zoya walked over. Rosie selected a sheath from a nearby bench, draped it over Zoya's shoulders and tightened it around her waist. Grasping Storm's handle, she wrenched the blade from the deck and slotted it into the sheath. She stepped back to admire her work. 'Dangerous,' she said.

'Now, have you used a sword before?'

'Never.'

'Good,' said Rosie. 'People are easier to teach when they're fresh. Now, draw!'

Zoya placed her right hand around the grip and lifted Storm from its sheath. She'd been telling the truth when she'd confessed to never holding a sword. She raised the blade until it was pointed horizontally away, her right arm level with her ears, elbow bent back, her other stretched across her chest so that her left hand jutted up against her right. She stared past her knuckles and concentrated on the sword's tip, surprised at its lack of weight. Zoya remained in this stance, breathing slowly. Rosie eyed her suspiciously.

'What?' asked Zoya, letting the blade drop. 'Am I doing it wrong?'

'No,' said Rosie, returning Zoya's arm. 'Not at all. You're doing it well. It's just . . .' she paused, seemingly elsewhere, '. . . your stance reminds me of someone.'

Zoya eyed Rosie, puzzled. But Rosie brushed aside the glance and motioned for Zoya to start. The younger girl needed no encouragement, and made a few exploratory movements with the sword, swiping and jabbing. Once she was convinced she could carry its weight, she brought it back in front of her and waited. Rosie cocked her head. 'Happy?'

Zoya nodded.

'Right, I'm going to attack. I want you to defend . . .'

Before Rosie finished her sentence, she lunged forward and swiped at Zoya's ear. Zoya dodged the attack just in time and spun around to face her, Storm at her side.

'Lesson two,' said Rosie, 'never drop your sword.'

Rosie brought hers round again, this time to bump Zoya on the shoulder. Zoya was prepared, and managed to evade the jab by rolling under the blade and springing back up with her sword in position. Rosie dashed to her right and sent in another shot—this one a little slower—which Zoya knocked aside, the clatter of metal ringing in her ear.

They continued like this, Rosie casually manoeuvring into position and firing an attack when Zoya least expected it. The younger girl matched Rosie most of the time, spinning to avoid her blows or ducking beneath them, jumping over them if they were aimed at her legs or even—when the chance arose—blocking a few. After a minute, she was panting and ready to collapse.

'Stop,' said Rosie, her breathing steady. 'You sure you haven't done this before?'

'Only with broom handles,' said Zoya.

'I think we need something more difficult.' Rosie disappeared into the corner of the room and returned with a pair of metal buckets. She tossed these into the centre of the mat. Next, she approached one of the benches, reached behind it and pulled out a long, wooden plank. 'Set those buckets down over there, would you?' she called to Zoya, nodding at two spots either side of the gym.

When Zoya had positioned the containers, Rosie hauled the plank of wood and balanced it across the buckets. 'Up you get,' she said.

Zoya looked to see if she was kidding.

'What?' said Rosie. 'The chances of you fighting someone on flat ground are slim. More likely, you'll be jumping up and down, ducking under things, rolling. If you can't block me whilst walking across this plank, how are you going to do any of that?'

'Let me get my breath back.'

'Would Kane?'

Rosie glared at Zoya until she picked up Storm. The girl reattached it to her waist then jumped onto the plank, which rocked a little on the buckets. Rosie started to stalk Zoya as she crossed the wood, jabbing with her sword whenever she thought Zoya close to falling, tipping her over the edge into a heap on the floor. She did this repeatedly, every so often catching Zoya with a blow across her arm or one of her thighs. Each time she fell, Zoya pushed herself off the ground and jumped back to the plank, ready for more. But such determination failed to mask her inability. On the ground, Zoya was as agile as a cat. On the plank, she was a turtle.

'Need a break?' asked Rosie, after yet another bruising fall.

'Break?' wheezed Zoya. 'This is amazing.'

Rosie chuckled and helped her back up. For the next hour they repeated the drill—Rosie stalking, Zoya fighting to keep her balance and eventually tumbling to the mat. As time passed, and as she came to understand the techniques required, Zoya started to block a few shots. It was only the easy ones at first—the ones Rosie pulled back from so as not to injure her—but they were blocks all the same and they caused Zoya to leap back onto the plank every time she fell in anticipation of getting it right.

Up and down she went, until after a couple of hours there were more ups than downs. Her positioning was still poor, but if she had a good grip on Storm and some idea of Rosie's location, she'd more likely block than take a hit.

Eventually, Rosie slotted her sword back into her scabbard and extended an arm for Zoya to climb down. In her bruised, sweating state, she didn't realize at first that it was over. When she did, she frowned.

'Not bad,' said Rosie. 'Not bad at all. You're done for today . . .'

Zoya moved to protest, but Rosie waved her away. 'I've been doing this for a long time. You're done. Next lesson is tomorrow morning.'

'I've got a cleaning shift tomorrow,' said Zoya, sucking in a lungful of air.

'Before that then,' said Rosie. 'I like to get up early.'

Zoya groaned, but a smile remained. It was still there when she left the gym and headed back up the stairs.

33

Rosie had worked Zoya so hard that the thought of food made her queasy, and she stayed on deck as the rest of the crew made their way inside for supper. A couple of other pirates remained—a man sitting on a barrel reading in the moonlight and a woman plucking a fiddle. Their presence reminded Zoya of Kane's threatened return, and she examined the pair to make sure she'd seen them on the *Dragonfly* before she was able to relax.

Feeling guilty that she'd shirked the day's cleaning, Zoya grabbed a brush and started to sweep the decks. She lifted the brush every so often to practise one of the moves she'd learned in the gym, earning her a series of sidelong glances from the fiddling thief. In time, she spotted Bucker emerging from the mess hall, ready for his evening shift. She watched him leap onto the mainmast and pull himself up the rigging with just his arms. His fawn hair reflected the moonlight, reminding Zoya of an animal, lithe, graceful. She waited until he was seated, then made her way over.

'Hey!' she shouted. 'Want some company?'

Bucker's head appeared over the edge of the pod. He stared at her, then disappeared. Zoya started to wonder whether she'd done something to annoy him, when a puppet appeared in Bucker's place. Its eyes and lips were bright red, and set in a white, skull-face that reminded Zoya of the yearly 'fright' party Mr Whycherley held at the orphanage. 'What's the password?'

'Erm . . . Bucker's a dope.'

'No.'

Zoya thought again. 'Zoya's a dope.'

'Bingo. Come on up.'

Zoya shook her head, then started to climb. Her skills were still nowhere near Bucker's, although she had improved. She managed to make it up to the pod in less than a minute. Bucker was slouched down with a grin on his face, the puppet still in his hand. 'Did you get caught in traffic?' it said.

'That was quick!' defended Zoya.

'For a legless ant,' said Bucker. He laid the puppet down, then nodded at it. 'Cool, eh?'

'Kinda horrible,' said Zoya.

'He's not,' said Bucker, stroking the puppet. Zoya laughed as Bucker started to buzz around the pod, clearing away the things left behind by the old man with whom he shared the space. Zoya pulled herself up off the comfy chair and helped. 'Scary what happened this morning, eh?'

Zoya stopped and looked at Bucker to see if he was being serious. 'You weren't really scared.'

'Only a bit,' answered Bucker. 'Stuff like that happens pretty often when you're a sky thief. But you were.'

'No,' said Zoya.

'You were. You nearly jumped out of your skin. I'm surprised there's any left.' Bucker pinched Zoya's forearm.

'Cut it out,' said Zoya. She frowned. 'OK, I was a bit scared. You would be too, if Kane was after you.'

'Maybe,' said Bucker. 'But I wouldn't show it.'

'I'm a kid,' said Zoya. 'Of course I show it.'

'Well, you can't. The quickest way to beat someone is to frighten them into thinking you've already won. That's what Kane's trying to do.'

Zoya didn't know what to say, so she said nothing. Dinner was over and the deck was busy again. There were dozens of thieves milling about in the moonlight. 'I heard you trained with Mum this afternoon,' continued Bucker.

'Yes.'

'She's the best.'

'So I hear,' said Zoya. 'It was hard.'

'Fun, though?'

Zoya nodded.

'Are you training with her again?'

'Before work tomorrow,' said Zoya.

'Listen to her,' said Bucker. 'You never know when you're

going to have to fight on an airship.'

Zoya rubbed her forehead. 'I thought I was tough, but I'm a long way off.'

'You'll get there,' said Bucker, flexing his biceps. 'They said that about me when I first got here. Now look.' He kissed the right muscle, then the left.

Zoya giggled. But as she did, her smile tipped to a frown. 'Oh,' she said.

Bucker dropped his arms. 'What's up?'

'Erm . . .' Zoya nodded over Bucker's shoulder. 'It's just weird. The sails are flapping up.'

Bucker rolled his eyes. 'Flapping up? Oh boy, it's going to be a long time before you pick up the lingo.'

'No, seriously,' said Zoya.

With a groan, Bucker pulled himself up to the edge of the pod and peered down at the sails. A puzzled expression appeared on his face. 'How strange.'

'What is it?' asked Zoya.

Bucker inhaled. 'Well, either gravity's reversed direction,' he said, 'or we're starting to descend.'

34

As the minutes passed, and the ship continued to drop, other crew members started to notice their new course. One rushed to the gunwale just as Zoya and Bucker landed back on the deck. 'We're definitely sinking,' said the thief.

'You've sank enough ale!' said another.

'No seriously. Come look.'

Others came to the same conclusion. Soon, a rumour started to spread that the ship was under attack, and people rushed about the deck trying to locate their pursuers. When no one could, they marched up to Cid, manning the bridge, and demanded to know what was happening. All Cid would say was 'orders from the boss.' When they asked him for more, he shook his head.

The *Dragonfly* continued to descend. With each passing minute, more thieves emerged. One or two knocked on the captain's quarters, but Vaspine didn't answer and they soon gave up.

Eventually, the ship touched down in the centre of a large

meadow, hitting the ground with a bump before skidding to a stop. After a few seconds, Cid cut the engine and a silence overtook the craft. It was the first time the *Dragonfly* had landed since Zoya's arrival. She felt both strange and excited.

The door to Vaspine's quarters opened and the captain stepped out. Without catching anyone's eye, he ordered everyone off the ship and onto the ground. Something about his manner seemed to worry the crew—Zoya included—and they made their way down the gangplank quickly and quietly. Zoya managed to sneak a glance at Rosie, but she shrugged and shook her head to indicate that she, too, was in the dark.

The crew lined up neatly on the grass—some standing with arms folded, waiting to hear what the captain had to say, others sitting on the floor, running their hands through the grass and enjoying the novel sensation of being on the surface. Vaspine was the last to exit. He walked down the gangplank on his own, his face drawn. When he reached the bottom, he took up a position at the front. 'Thank you.'

The crowd released a tense burst of laughter.

Vaspine continued. 'I apologize for doing this in such a dramatic fashion. But I know many of you have questions about what happened this morning at the Aviation Army airbase, and I want to try to answer them.

'Zoya,' said Vaspine. 'You might as well come forward.'

Zoya blushed as everyone in the crowd faced her. She made her way through the tangle and up to the front.

'Most of you have met Zoya,' continued Vaspine. 'She joined our ship a few days ago. I expect some of you have asked about her past and she's answered you. I'm afraid her answers have been lies. Necessary lies, but lies nevertheless.' He looked at Zoya. 'So here's the truth: the girl Kane referred to in his message this morning is Zoya.'

An audible gasp escaped the crowd. They stared at the captain momentarily, then one or two started to look amongst each other, muttering questions. Somebody near the back shouted, 'But why?'

Vaspine took a breath. 'It's not a secret that Kane and I served with Jupiter and Dominika when we were younger.' He paused and laid a hand on Zoya's shoulder. 'And it's common knowledge Kane murdered them during his mutiny aboard the *White Knight*.'

There were nods of ascent.

'But what some of you might not know,' continued Vaspine, 'is that Jupiter had a baby girl. I managed to smuggle the girl off the ship before Kane made good on his scheme.' Vaspine glanced at Zoya, then back at the crowd. 'The girl stands before you now.'

There was another sharp intake of breath, then more mumbling. Vaspine waited for it to die, before continuing. 'As many of you are aware, Jupiter kept a vault hidden somewhere on the Island in the Sky. Not even his men knew its location. I do. So does Kane. The key to this vault was lost on the night of Kane's mutiny.' Vaspine paused. 'The key is the locket that hangs around Zoya's neck.'

Zoya felt an urge to run as the heat of the crowd turned her way once more. She calmed her breathing, and instead pulled out the chain and displayed it for them. They craned their heads to get a better look.

'This is why we had to bring Zoya on board, and it's also why Kane left us that message this morning. He wants the locket. And whilst we might be safe right now, he is coming. He's been chasing this thing for a decade. He won't give up. We mustn't let him have it.' Vaspine paused to let the words sink in. He looked around the crowd, meeting each of their eyes. 'Now, I didn't mean to get any of you into this. Risk is a part of the sky thief life. It's what we sign up for when we take to the skies. But this is a step too far. We're on the surface now. Any of you who wishes to, may leave. Gather your things. We've landed on the main road to Dalmacia, you can reach the city in a day. None of us will think any less of you. We all have families. It wouldn't do for any more little boys and girls to grow up alone.'

There was a murmuring. Zoya glanced at Bucker, who smiled. After a minute, a few people made their way forward.

'I'm sorry cap', I have to . . .'

'My wife already hates me for doing this job . . .'

The last of them studiously avoided Zoya's gaze. When he arrived at the captain, he leaned into Vaspine's ear. 'You know I'd rob fat cats with you until the end of time cap', but I didn't join up to fight Kane. Not him.' He flicked his eyes across to Zoya, then lowered them again. His voice dropped to a whisper, 'I'm sorry . . .'

The captain shook his hand. 'You don't have to apologize. Think nothing of it. You can return when this is over.'

The man trudged up the gangplank and back onto the ship. Vaspine watched him until he disappeared, then returned his attention to those on the grass. 'Anyone else?'

No one moved.

35

Many crew members had questions, so it was late by the time they made their way back to the airship. Some lingered on the ground a while longer, excited to have their feet on solid earth. The rest bunched in small groups on deck, sharing an ale and discussing the news as Cid set the *Dragonfly* in the direction of the Dalmacia Pass and gunned the engines. Zoya stayed out with them, doing her best to bear the constant attention and trying to keep up her spirits. But it was tough. Kane was still out there. Somewhere in the skies his airship was lurking, slithering through the darkness.

'Are you OK?' asked Bucker, running into her as he darted across the deck. In his hands he carried a felt bag.

Zoya forced a smile. 'I'm just tired,' she said.

'You should come and play cards,' said Bucker. 'Take your mind off it. There's a few of us down by the mainmast. Pontoon.'

'Now?' asked Zoya. She glanced down the deck, where Beebee and a couple of other thieves were gathered around a fold-up table. 'They'd play with me?'

'Course,' said Bucker. 'You don't think you're the only one on this ship with a secret, do you? Every single pirate here's had a run in with one sky thief or another.' He smiled a toothy smile. 'Your man's just . . . bigger.'

'Mmm.'

'Have you got any money?' asked Bucker as they walked to the mainmast.

Zoya shook her head.

'Doesn't matter. Herman Bernard will lend you some. That OK, Herman?'

Herman rolled his eyes. 'For Jupiter's daughter,' he said, 'no problem.'

'Well,' said Bucker, impatiently, 'sit!' He pulled out a chair for Zoya, then proceeded to introduce the final thief. 'Zoya meet James 'Piggy Bank' Jones. We call him that because he's like a piggy bank. Whenever any of us want any money, we play James at cards.'

Zoya took a roll of coins from Herman Bernard, thanked him and submerged herself in the game, trying to forget Kane. After obliterating everyone in the first hand (she was sure Bucker had fixed the cards), her luck spiralled. The next hand she lost terribly, betting way more than she should and losing all of her recently acquired winnings. The following hand was also a nightmare. She did middling on the one after that, then lost the next worse than all the others combined.

Bucker, alternatively, won nearly every hand he played. Zoya concluded that she'd already lost more than she'd ever gain, so she spent the next few hands watching Bucker closely to work out what he was doing to be so successful. At first, she didn't notice anything in particular. He appeared to be doing precisely the things Zoya was—betting, checking, calling, betting again. But then she noticed something peculiar: every time Bucker was dealt a new hand of cards, he'd lean down beneath the table and scratch his feet. He always said something as he did this, whether it was 'ouch' or 'my feet are really itchy,' or pointing towards another crew member on the ship doing something silly. Nevertheless, every time he received a new set of cards, his hands would go down to his feet.

The next time Zoya noticed this, she rocked backwards and forwards in her chair until she tipped over and fell to the floor. She made it look like an accident, of course, but it wasn't. From the floor, she had a good view underneath the table. Sure enough, she spotted Bucker's hand groping around the deck, where he kept a secret stash of Kings and Queens. *Got you*.

Bucker was the first to leap down off his chair and help her up. As he did, he caught her eye. Gleaming there was a spark of recognition. She knew. He knew she knew. He whispered in her ear as he set her back in her seat. 'Shhh.'

A couple of rounds later, Bucker announced that he needed the toilet and skipped off in the direction of the

141

nearest lavatory, leaving Zoya alone with the others. For a few seconds nobody spoke. Zoya started to feel prickly, and wanted to run back to her room. Then, James 'Piggy Bank' Jones leaned under the table and said, 'let's have a look what he's got today.' He pulled out Bucker's stashed cards and slapped them face-up on the table. The others looked them over, then murmured to each other, 'Oooh, he could have played that when . . .' and, ' Now *that* would have made a good finisher two rounds ago . . .' and, 'Oh well, he'll get it one day!'

Zoya watched perplexed, before she had to speak. 'You know he cheats?'

Beebee and the others turned their heads slowly towards her. Zoya felt like she'd said something wrong. She was about to break the tension with a quip when James spoke. 'Zoya, a blind monkey with no ears and half a brain would know he cheats.'

Zoya looked confused. 'Then why do you let him get away with it?'

The man cocked his head and considered how best to put it. 'You see him over there?' he said, referring to a crew member sitting on top of a bucket and picking his lunch out of his teeth. 'I've known him for ten years. And you see him?' He pointed to another flexing his muscles in the reflection of a metal crate.

Zoya nodded.

'Seven.' The others nodded in agreement. 'I know the men around this table like I know my own feet, and that ain't good. There's not a single thing any one of them can tell me that I haven't heard before.' The man noticed Bucker making his way back from the toilet and dropped his cards beneath the table. He looked up at Zoya. 'When Bucker came on board this ship, he was like a lantern in the night. That boy could cheat me out of a hundred coins and it'd still be a cheap price to pay for his company.'

36

When Bucker arrived back at the table, he noticed everyone staring. 'What?' he asked, glancing down at his trousers to make sure they were buttoned. He threw his hands into the air. 'What?'

No one said anything, then Zoya answered. 'Nothing,' she said with a smile. 'Let's play on.'

Bucker checked his trousers again to be sure, then sat down. He gathered up the cards from the table and dealt a new hand, two cards to each player. James Jones winked at Zoya when he knew Bucker wasn't looking. Zoya nodded in return.

They carried on playing for another hour, switching to a different game halfway through to 'give us a chance,' as Herman Bernard put it. As it was, they fared no better in the second game. By the end of the hour, Bucker had cleaned up all of their money save for one or two coins Zoya had managed to cling onto. After another victorious hand, Bucker rose out of his chair and started to gather his winnings. 'I'd love to stay here and take all the coins in your pockets,' he said, 'but I've got a shift in the lookout. Save up some more gold and I'll take if off you next time, OK?'

Beebee, Herman, and James rolled their eyes.

The game drew to a close. Herman and James thanked Zoya and Beebee, then wandered shakily down the ship, swinging bottles of wine. Beebee watched them and shook his head. 'You're lucky Zo,' he said. 'They might look like a couple of over-liquored reprobates, but we've got a good crew here. A lot of thieves would up and run away if Kane was after them. Not the *Dragonfly*.'

Beebee started to tidy away the card table and chucked a box to Zoya so she could gather up the cards, money bags, cigarette trays and ale bottles. When she'd finished, she bent to lift the box. As she dug her fingers beneath the cardboard, she realized for the first time just how exhausted she was. Rosie's training had sapped the last of her strength, and she felt as insubstantial as a ghost. Seeing this, Beebee chuckled, then nodded for Zoya to grab the table as he lifted the box.

Zoya's eyelids started to droop as together they stumbled down the airship. At one point, she nearly bumped into a pair of passing thieves, who pirouetted to avoid her. The sky around them was pitch-black now, so that the few lanterns cast fuzzy shadows on the *Dragonfly's* deck. Off in the distance, flashes of light lanced the sky, accompanied by

145

muffled *whumps*. The crew left on the deck tried to see what was happening. Beebee leaned in. 'You all right?'

Zoya looked up. As she did, she heard a loud *fizzuuup*, then a sharp cracking sound. Looking about, Zoya half expected to see the red face of a thief scrambling about the deck, trying to gather up what they'd dropped. But there was nobody. Instead, the entire crew had frozen and were staring at Beebee. Zoya gazed at them, puzzled, then at Beebee. The big man was looking into the cardboard box. Zoya followed his gaze and gasped. Where before had been the card-game paraphernalia was now a smoking chunk of rock the size of Zoya's fist. The heat charred the cardboard and sent smoke billowing into Beebee's eyes. A look of confusion registered on his face as he tried to work out what had happened.

It was then that he and Zoya heard another crash to their left, and looked across to see a smoking hole in the middle of the deck. This was followed by another crash ahead of them, then another right by Zoya's feet.

'What's going . . .' Zoya started, but before she could finish a shout from a nearby thief answered her question.

'Meteors!'

37

Zoya located the main body of the shower—a storm of light around a mile ahead. Hundreds of fireballs flashed diagonally across the sky, with crystal heads and tails that sparked briefly before disappearing. The meteors were beautiful, in spite of the danger, as if the sky was raining light. Zoya stood mesmerized, until she was jolted back to life as another meteor crashed through the gunwale and lodged in the deck near her feet. Zoya searched for Beebee and found him further down the deck. 'What should I do?' she shouted.

'Get under cover!'

Zoya scanned the deck for somewhere strong enough to withstand a falling meteor. She thought about descending into the cargo holds, but nearly everything on the *Dragonfly* was made of wood. If a meteor crashed through the top deck it would almost certainly crash through the lower decks too. The little metal on the ship was either clamped to the hull and inaccessible, or so high above the deck that trying to get there would be suicide.

Thinking of height made Zoya think of Bucker, and she glanced over to his lookout pod to see if he was there. From a distance, it was clear his pod was intact, although the nearby rigging had blasted apart, leaving a huge hole in the middle. Zoya ran over. 'Bucker?'

Bucker's head appeared over the edge of the pod. 'I can't get down. A meteor's hit the netting.'

'I can see,' yelled Zoya, as another meteor whistled through the air and crashed into the mainmast, making her drop to the floor. She jumped back up a second later and checked the mast, which smoked briefly but failed to catch fire. Zoya looked to where she'd last seen Bucker, but he was gone. Surveying the area, she found him again, far from the pod, hanging in the air off a crossbeam.

'How did you . . . ?'

'It threw me,' said Bucker. 'Get me down!'

Zoya searched the deck for something to help. She needed rope, but Vaspine kept all the cord at the ship's bow, and she knew she wouldn't make it there and back before Bucker fell. She pushed aside rice sacks and wine barrels to try to find some, but there was nothing. Off to her right, Zoya spotted Beebee trying to lift a wooden beam that had fallen onto Charlie. Zoya darted over, grabbed a corner and lifted. As she hoisted, she asked Beebee if he'd seen any rope.

'Zoya, I'm busy!'

Between them, they managed to haul the beam off

Charlie and hurl it across the deck. Zoya raced back to Bucker, frantically searching as she ran.

'I can't find anything,' she shouted.

'Hurry!' said Bucker. 'If I die, I am so going to haunt you.'

Zoya surveyed everything around her once more—sacks, barrels, tables, masts—and started to form a plan. She grabbed a couple of sacks, dragged them until they were beneath Bucker, then returned and did the same until she'd built up a pile. Next, she manoeuvred barrels into position around the sacks to hold them in place, and looked up.

'You're kidding,' said Bucker.

'Best I can do. Now jump!'

Bucker closed his eyes, counted to three and let go. He plummeted through the air and landed on the sacks with a *thud*. Zoya looked down to see if he was OK just in time to receive a well-timed jab to her arm. 'That's the last time I ask you to save me,' said Bucker.

Together, they returned the sacks to the side of the ship. When they'd finished, Bucker brushed his hands free of dust. 'We need to find my mum.'

They ran to the centre deck and started to search for Rosie. It was Zoya who recognized her first, striding up the deck behind a furious-looking Vaspine.

'Mum!' shouted Bucker.

Rosie's head jerked around at the sound of her son's voice, and a look of irritation warped her face. She strode over, grabbed him and Zoya by their shirts and dragged them across the deck towards the captain. Together, they stormed to the rear of the ship, the kids stumbling to keep up. 'Stay by my side,' she hissed.

When they arrived at the stern, Vaspine leapt onto the bridge where Cid was wrestling with the wheel, lurching the ship left and right to avoid the biggest of the meteors. Rosie strode to the side wall and ran a finger along the edge until it caught on a catch. She hooked her fingers around it and pulled. From beneath the lip extended a metal lid, which revealed a gap just large enough to shelter Zoya and Bucker. 'Get in there and don't move.'

The kids crawled inside and positioned the lid above their heads. Rosie turned around and leapt onto the bridge.

'Cid,' said Vaspine, 'what's your plan?'

The pilot winked. 'Same as always.'

Cid returned his attention to the storm—the heart of which, Zoya noticed, was now alarmingly close. Dozens of meteors blasted through the hull every minute. They no longer seemed as beautiful as they had from afar.

'Captain,' shouted Zoya. 'Are we going to be OK?'

Vaspine smiled. 'Two things could happen, Zoya. This man,' he pointed at Cid, 'will fly us out of this mess. Or the *Dragonfly* will get hit by one too many of these peanuts and we'll smash to the ground. Now, be quiet and let us work.'

38

Cid spun the wheel until the ship was zooming through the sky. The wind rushed past the hull, deafening Zoya, and the meteors that hit the ship exploded in a shower of sparks. There were hundreds now, some as tiny as peas, others as large as apples, bursting through the clouds with small puffs. The rocks battered some clouds more than others, and Zoya figured this was how Cid was keeping them safe—using the clouds to gauge where the shower was most violent and steering them in the opposite direction. Near the storm's centre the meteors grew to the size of melons that would have sent the ship spiralling had they stuck in the wrong place. But they didn't. And somehow, Cid managed to carve a path through. Slowly, the sky ahead started to clear. And after another minute of careful flying, the *Dragonfly* was free.

Zoya grabbed Bucker and pulled him out of their hole. Together, they surveyed the ship. Zoya had never seen anything like it. The *Dragonfly* was almost unrecognizable. Small fires raged everywhere, sending clouds of smoke into the sky. Entire chunks of deck were missing, either smashed and splintered, or pocked by so many holes that they looked like a sieve. Bucker glanced up at the area around his lookout pod and found it pulverized, the ship's sails shredded and torn. Even the crew's quarters, towards the ship's bow, had not been spared.

Cid ordered the more experienced crew members about, including sending Bucker up to what remained of his pod to be on the lookout for any more unwelcome surprises ('if you see even the hint of a black and red ship, you shout me!'). Zoya took the chance to visit the injured in a hastily-built hospital near the engine room. The captain was there when she arrived, moving between beds fashioned out of desks and sofas, telling jokes or tales of his injuries down the years.

Zoya made her own journey around the beds, trying to cheer the injured patients with chunks of cake she'd smuggled out of the mess hall. When she'd finished, she headed back out to the deck to see if there was anything else she could do to help. Instead, she found her attention drawn to a clump of people beneath the mainmast. Cid was there, and Rosie and the captain too, their arms locked across their chests. 'What do you mean we've got nothing?' barked Vaspine.

'Exactly what I say,' said Cid. He pressed a wad of tobacco into his pipe and struck a match in the dark. 'We've lost one of the sails. She ain't flying.'

'At all?'

'Oh, she'd beat a snail,' said Cid, 'but don't arrange any dinner dates for the next few days—we ain't going to make them.'

'How fast can we go, Cid?'

The pilot scrunched up his face. 'I'd say we're as quick as a transporter. Maybe.'

'A transporter!' Vaspine stared at the pilot, his face grim, then looked up at the sails. Cid was telling the truth when he'd suggested one of the sails had survived intact, and it hung above them as always, obscuring the stars. But the one nearest Bucker's lookout had been hammered. Its top half was punctured across its entire breadth, and strips of its shredded lower section drooped to the deck like spaghetti.

'So we fix it,' said the captain, simply. He approached Rosie, who was still observing the damaged sail. 'The Doc left us some of the fabric, right?'

Rosie swung her head slowly down. 'Not enough. We used a bunch of it after we hit that bridge last year.'

'Damn it,' said Vaspine. He kicked a wooden bucket across the deck. 'So what do we do? We can't get to the Dalmacia Pass if we're slower than a transporter. What about the city? Say we head down, pick up some sails and patch her up?'

Cid and Rosie exchanged a glance. Rosie stepped forward. 'Carlos, it took the Doc a year to put these things together. Even if Dalmacia did sell the stuff,' she raised a finger, 'which I don't think it does, no one on board could fix it. We need to get to the pass *now*, not in weeks.'

Vaspine shook his head. 'We're not getting him.'

'Who?'

'I know what you two are thinking. It's not going to happen.'

Cid finished his pipe, tapped out the ash and slotted it back into his jacket. When he was done, he conjured his gold coin and started to manipulate it between his fingers. 'The way I see it, we've got one working sail. We can't repair the other, which means we've got to get some more juice out of that one. And unless Zoya's some kid genius . . .' he turned to Zoya and extended a hand, waiting for an answer. Zoya shook her head. '. . . Then I'd say unless we plan on sitting here and waiting for Kane, the Doc's our only option.'

Vaspine bared his teeth. He looked at Rosie. 'You agree?'

She shrugged. 'He's always right.'

Cid laughed.

'Goddamn,' said Vaspine, already walking back to his cabin. He looked over his shoulder. 'Please tell me we're close.'

Cid pushed himself upright. 'That's where you're in luck. If we can keep this tailwind, we'll be at the coast in a day. Maybe less.'

'A day!' Vaspine started, but managed to compose himself. 'OK. Do it. But, goddamn, be on the lookout for that ship. If Kane finds us when we can't fly, we're done. Quiet as a mouse, Cid.'

The pilot flashed a grin. 'Squeak squeak.'

39

Zoya had forgotten to make her bed that morning, which made it all the easier to dive straight in when she eventually went to sleep. Zoya did this, pulling the covers over her and making a pocket of darkness. She lay still for a while, thinking of everything that had happened. Kane's message, the meteor strike. It was like the sky was conspiring against her. And yet, the way the crew had reacted to the captain's announcement gave her hope. If they were behind her, she at least stood a chance.

The sun was streaming in through a hole in her roof when she woke in the morning. It was still early, and she threw on her clothes and padded out to the deck. Charlie and Maddie were already up, outside the mess hall, serving bacon cobs from a trolley. Zoya joined the queue. When she reached the front, she asked Charlie why they were outside. 'There are so many holes in that mess hall it might as well be a cheese-grater!'

By the time Zoya had finished her breakfast, a group of thieves had formed outside the crew's quarters. Bucker was there, and he raced over as soon as he saw Zoya. He hooked his arm into hers. 'Enjoy your lie-in?'

'What's going on?' asked Zoya.

'We're waiting for the captain. We're the clean-up crew. We're going to fill in the meteor holes.'

'How?'

'However. Most, we'll repair with wood. Others,' Bucker smiled as he said this, 'will require a little more attention.'

Before Zoya could ask what he meant, the captain emerged from below deck and approached the crowd. 'I appreciate you all meeting me here,' he said. 'As I'm sure one of my loudest little birds has told you,' he flashed a smile at Bucker, 'you're going to be my clean-up team. Fetching though it is, with Kane over our shoulder we can't have the *Dragonfly* looking like this for long. I want you people to spend the morning scouring the ship for rocks, holes, damage – anything that might cause a problem—and fix them.'

'Can Zoya join us?' blurted Bucker.

Vaspine glanced at Zoya. 'If she wishes.'

The captain spent the next twenty minutes briefing the team about what he wanted. After that, he left them to get on, promising a substantial lunch if they could finish the job by the afternoon. Once he'd gone, Zoya turned to Bucker. 'Now what?'

Bucker was fighting through the crowd to get the best equipment. She watched him elbow people aside like a terrier, grabbing what he could before someone else snatched it up. 'Now,' he smiled, when he was done, 'we have fun.'

40

Zoya and Bucker picked their way around the cavernous holes that had wrecked the bow and stern of the ship and headed towards the central deck where most of the damage comprised small, fist-sized holes. Fixing these involved removing the remaining meteor shards that had lodged either side, throwing these off the airship, selecting an appropriate length of wood from a nearby pile, covering the hole and nailing it into position. 'This isn't a long-term fix, is it?' asked Zoya.

Bucker shook his head. 'Next time we touch down we'll get one of the shipyards to fix her up proper.' He beat a final nail into the plank at his knees and lobbed his hammer into the air. 'But the more we get done before your friend returns, the better.'

They continued their repairs for the next hour, inching their way up the deck every few minutes when they'd cleared a patch. Periodically, Cid would wander by on his way up to the bridge to check there had been no sightings of Kane.

'Nothing?' asked Zoya, after one of these trips.

'Nothing,' said Cid, winking. 'He's not stupid. He's heard who the *Dragonfly*'s pilot is.'

She knew Cid was kidding around to make her feel better, but it *did* make her feel better, so she appreciated it all the same.

Once Bucker had finished hammering the final nail into his sixteenth hole of the morning, he lifted his head. 'Snack?'

'Snack,' agreed Zoya.

They made their way to Bucker's cabin, where he brought out some chunks of chocolate he'd pilfered from the mess hall a few days before. The squares were speckled white here and there, but Zoya didn't mind, and she wolfed down the pieces hungrily. When they'd finished, they made their way back out onto deck. Already huddled there were the rest of the clean-up team. Zoya and Bucker crept through the bodies until they could hear what was being said.

'That brings us to the hull,' said the old man in charge. 'Now, unfortunately, I'm too old to be jumping off airships, so I need some younger volunteers. Hands up.'

Before anyone else could raise their hands, Bucker thrust his and Zoya's into the air. 'We'll do it,' he shouted. Zoya yanked his hand to get it down, but Bucker held firm. 'We'll do it!'

The old man glanced at them. 'I know you've jumped before, but what about her?' He nodded at Zoya.

'Oh yeah,' said Bucker, 'she's jumped a hundred times.'

Zoya whispered the word 'no' under her breath. The old man eyed them, then turned to the rest of the crowd. 'Well, if the captain thinks they're sharp enough to be part of the clean-up team, they're sharp enough to know if they want to jump off an airship. OK, who else?'

As the old man canvassed for more volunteers, Bucker dragged Zoya towards the side of the airship. He stood before her with a grin.

'Did he just say "jump off an airship?"'

'You can thank me later.' Bucker winked.

'Thank you?'

'Yes! The wind rushing through your hair, the feeling you're falling into the centre of the planet. It's the best.'

'It sounds like the worst,' said Zoya. She visualized jumping off the ship. The thought took her back to her first night on the airship. 'Bucker, we don't have to do this.'

'You don't have to do anything,' said Bucker. 'You could sit in your pants all day and wait for Kane to come. Or you can go out into the fresh air, do something you've never done before and take your mind off it.' Bucker surprised himself with his passion and took a breath. 'Now,' he said, 'are you going to be a wimp, or are you going to come with me and jump off this ship?'

'If I'm a wimp, will you ever let me forget?'

'Nope.'

'In which case,' said Zoya, trying to sound enthusiastic, 'let's go!'

41

Zoya followed Bucker across the deck and down the passage next to Vaspine's quarters. When they arrived at the bow, he led her to a large wooden chest beneath the ship's figurehead. From out of this they each grabbed a heavy, metal clamp and some rope. The clamp was so weighty Zoya could barely lift it. 'Where are we jumping from?'

'Mum doesn't like me doing this,' said Bucker, 'so from wherever she won't see us.'

He led them across the deck and stopped just short of the side, not far from the figurehead and angled so as to be hidden from the rest of the ship. Bucker dropped his clamp and ropes to the floor. Zoya did the same, then started to unravel the long rope she'd wound around her body. Bucker helped by grabbing the free end and pulling until Zoya spun wildly.

'The rope's elasticated,' he said, once Zoya had regained equilibrium. 'But when you bounce that first time it's going to hurt. This is your clamp. What you do is place the metal side down on one of these,' Bucker slammed the clamp onto a nearby bracket, 'and the magnetic force will keep it in place.' He smirked. 'Hopefully.'

Zoya lifted her clamp, staggered with it to the nearest bracket and followed Bucker's instructions. When the clamp locked into position, Zoya grabbed it with two hands and tugged as hard as she could. It held. 'How does it come off?'

'It takes three people per clamp, but don't worry about that. The next thing you do,' said Bucker, demonstrating as he explained, 'is attach the linking end of the rope to the clamp, and the looped end around your waist.'

Zoya did the same, then looked over the edge of the gunwale. The sun had climbed high now, beating down on the deck and highlighting a bright sky smeared with wispy white clouds. She surveyed the landscape below — remote houses, hamlets, villages, towns. Near to the surface a few flying transporters ferried people here and there.

'Ready?' asked Bucker.

'No,' said Zoya.

'Oh well.' Bucker made his way up onto the side of the ship, shifting a bag of tools on his back. 'Right, I'll jump first. You need to watch how far I jump out and do exactly the same. That's important, because if you jump less you're going to hit the hull. You don't want that.' He adjusted the hoop around his waist. 'I'm going on three. See you down there.'

Bucker counted to three and jumped. He leapt as far as he could from the ship, leading with his hands as if he was diving into a lake. Zoya watched him shrink, the colour draining from his clothes until he was little more than a dot. The rope beside her rushed by until it reached its end, then yanked against the clamp. From somewhere below, Zoya heard a faint 'umphhh.'

Here goes. She took a last look over the edge, closed her eyes and jumped. Immediately, a wave of panic surged through her as the wind whipped past her face and tossed her clothes. Zoya thrust out her arms as Bucker had done and fought to open her eyes. She managed it eventually, and was overwhelmed by the patchwork ground growing in her field of vision. A moment later, she spotted Bucker's rope to her left, then Bucker below. At the same time, Zoya's own rope caught. She felt a sharp tug at her waist and then the curious sensation of falling upwards, the rope coiling around her. She bounced a few more times, then realized she could take in the view properly for the first time. The surface looked much like it had from the ship—the people there no more aware of Zoya and Bucker than they were of the clouds. It was only when Zoya turned around and caught sight of the *Dragonfly* that she had to gasp.

It was breathtaking.

Seeing the ship from below, Zoya realized how precarious their position really was. So much had happened since her rescue from the orphanage, so many surprising and frightening things, that she'd never considered what it meant to be living on an airship. Seeing its dark outline against the sun, she realized how small the *Dragonfly* really was, how exposed they were.

Zoya waited for her rope to stop bouncing, before steadying her feet on the hull. She spotted Bucker a few feet away and smiled. He smiled back. 'Enjoy?'

'That,' said Zoya, 'was awesome.'

42

In spite of the buffeting wind, fixing holes in the hull proved to be easier than fixing those up on deck. Avoiding dropping to their knees every time they wanted to position a piece of wood meant a lot less grazes and a lot more fun. Every so often, with the buzz of a fresh jump still fizzing through her veins, Zoya would hang motionless and just stare. She could see everything. Never before had she been able to see so much at once—cruisers, transporters, rivers, canals, forests, mountains, oceans, farms, birds, and all manner of things.

After a while, Zoya spotted a huge, dark spire creeping over the horizon. At first, it appeared to be an isolated building, a tower in the middle of nowhere. But as the *Dragonfly* drifted on, the spire blossomed into a sprawling city—the biggest she'd ever seen. Perched on a vast, rocky outcrop that stretched miles inland from the ocean, the city belched great plumes of smoke, creating a dense cloud in the sky above. Leading to the city's main gate was a winding stone path, dotted with towered checkpoints, each with its own queue of people. Peeling away from the front gate were two enormous stone walls that circled the city, forming a shield. Into these were carved colossal airports, providing access to the hundreds of airships buzzing around outside.

A cruiser, similar in size to the one they'd raided, slid through the centre of one of these ports before being swallowed by the city as if it was no bigger than a fly. 'Where's that?' she asked.

Bucker, who hadn't yet noticed the city, spun in his harness. 'Oh,' his face brightened, 'that's Dalmacia. We must be getting close to the Doc.'

'Dalmacia,' repeated Zoya. She shook her head, amazed she'd ever see such a place.

For the rest of the morning, they plugged as many of the holes as they could in their section of the hull and watched the city slide by. By the time they'd finished, the sun had disappeared behind a bank of clouds, streaming out from behind in thin, sharp shafts. It was a view Zoya found both beautiful and unsettling. And in spite of the morning's fun, she couldn't help remembering that Kane was out there somewhere.

'Want to go inside?' asked Bucker, noticing her frown.

'I think that's a good idea,' said Zoya.

The rest of the clean-up crew had made sure to repair the mess hall first ('you can't fight on an empty stomach!'), and Charlie and Maddie had moved back inside. Zoya made her way there for a plate of eggs, then returned to the deck, looking for distractions to take her mind off things. Aside from the usual lookouts and deputy pilots, there was only one other figure on deck besides Zoya, whose silhouette she could see leaning over the starboard gunwale. Zoya positioned herself behind what remained of the mainmast and watched them, thinking of Kane's threatened return.

She realized it was Beebee at the same time Beebee noticed her. He motioned her over. 'I was supposed to get a message to you. Where've you been?'

'Fixing the hull,' said Zoya.

Beebee's face cracked to a smirk. 'Rather you than me. Anyway, the captain wants you to meet him at the bow at three.'

'Me?' said Zoya.

Beebee nodded.

'What for?'

'Don't know. You'll find out, I guess.'

Zoya tried to imagine what might be happening at three, but was distracted by Beebee, who turned away and slumped onto a stool. Next to the seat was a bucket of soapy water and a rag. Beebee plunged his arm into the water, pulled it out and proceeded to wipe it with the cloth. At first, Zoya wondered what he was doing, but as she moved closer she realized Beebee was injured. A ring of crimson grazes corkscrewed around his arm from his wrist to his elbow.

168

Beebee patted them with the cloth, rinsing after every rub.

'What happened?' asked Zoya.

'Oh, nothing,' said Beebee. 'I was helping pull down the damaged sail when one of the cross-beams broke and fell.' Beebee held out his arm and angled it so Zoya could see. The skin was crimson, flecked with patches of angry, bruised purple.

'Wow.'

'It's all right,' said Beebee. 'Won't be boxing for a few days, though.'

Zoya smiled as Beebee thrust his hand back into the water. 'I know,' she said, 'how about I teach you how to feed the birds now? Wait here.'

Zoya ran to the food store at the airship's bow, located a sack of sunflower seeds, stuffed a handful into her pockets and raced back. 'With your deep voice, you're never going to get one to land on you by mimicking them like I did.'

Beebee nodded.

'So you need seeds.'

'Bird seeds?'

'Yes.'

Beebee rolled his eyes. 'Zoya, I know I don't have much up here,' he tapped his head, 'but do you really think I haven't tried a bird-feeder?'

Zoya wagged a finger. 'I don't mean a bird-feeder. Come on.'

Beebee hooked his injured arm into his waistcoat and followed Zoya, who led him across deck to the airship's stern. There were two birds there—both sparrows—fluttering and chirping whenever they found solid ground. As Zoya neared them, she motioned for Beebee to stay back. She tiptoed forwards, scattering seeds every so often. When she was close to the nearest bird, Zoya retraced her steps and dropped to one knee. She scattered a few seeds into her hand and laid it palm-up on the ground.

Then she waited.

It took a moment for the birds to notice the seeds. When they did, they eyed them with suspicion. After a second, any misgivings disappeared and they leaned in and started to peck. When the first pile had gone, they raised their heads and searched for more. Sure enough, they noticed the next handful and fluttered into position.

'Is this going to work?' whispered Beebee.

'Shhh!' said Zoya.

Pile by pile, the birds gobbled up the seeds until they were right by Zoya's hand. Without moving her body, she rocked her arm, causing the seeds to rustle. The birds heard this and snapped their heads. Noticing the seeds, they eyed Zoya cautiously, then hopped onto her hands. 'Quick,' whispered Zoya, 'grab some.'

Zoya rose with the birds in her cupped palm and edged towards Beebee, who was standing perfectly still, his hand filled with seeds. One of the birds, spotting the larger pile in Beebee's hand, hopped off Zoya's palm and onto Beebee's. A smile blossomed on the big man's face as he stood with a bird in his palm for the first time. 'Told you we'd do it,' whispered Zoya to Beebee, who was busy peering at the creature. 'Now, all you need to do is learn how to do it yourself and you'll be able to talk to all the birds you want.'

'I owe you one,' whispered Beebee.

Zoya thought back to the night Beebee had saved her from jumping off the airship and chuckled. 'No you don't,' she said. 'I'd say that makes us about even.'

43

Captain Vaspine and Cid were already at the bow when Zoya arrived, leaning against the transporter. The sun hung pin-sharp in the sky. Curls of smoke from Cid's pipe merged with wisps of breath from the captain. When the pilot saw Zoya, he tapped the remaining ash from his pipe and nodded. 'Her ladyship arrives.'

'Hey,' said Zoya, 'I'm early.'

The captain elbowed Cid from his position against the transporter and started to unstrap the craft from its moorings, gesturing for Zoya to help him. Zoya had never seen a transporter in daylight, and she regarded it closely. The craft was an oblong hunk of metal, about the size of a dining table. Inside were six seats—three in front and three at the back—along with an array of levers. 'What's going on?' she asked.

'We're nearly at the Doc's,' said the captain. 'We're going to leave the *Dragonfly* here and go the rest of the way in one of these. Less chance of being spotted.'

'You want me to come?'

The captain started to hand Zoya objects to load into the back of the craft—backpacks, food, tools, his dagger, a spyglass. 'The Doc left us a year ago,' he explained. 'We had a falling out. He went to set up a lab in a village just down the coast.' He gestured towards the ground. 'Trust me, I'd love to leave him stewing there, but unfortunately he's the best at what he does. If we want to have a chicken's chance of getting away from Kane, we need his help . . . and we need you to talk him into it.'

'But I've never met him,' said Zoya.

'Oh, few have,' said Vaspine, circling the transporter and ducking every few feet to check the underside of the craft. 'Even on the *Dragonfly* he spent all of his time below deck. But that might work in your favour. The Doc won't talk to me. Let's just say he knows how to hold a grudge. Has Bucker told you anything about him?'

'He told me his name.'

Vaspine shrugged. 'He has a real name, but it's best to call him the Doc. He's a curious man, exceedingly clever.'

'How can I convince him?' asked Zoya.

The captain stopped in front of her. 'The Doc knew your parents, Zoya. He served under them on their first ship. I'm hoping when he finds out you're their daughter, it might sway him into coming back.'

'And if not?'

Vaspine reached into the back of the transporter and lifted a money bag. The coins *plinked* against each other. 'If not, we try coin.'

The captain snapped a finger for Zoya to get into the transporter, then levered himself into the pilot seat. As they strapped themselves in, Cid approached the captain, then looked past him and smiled at Zoya. 'Don't look so worried, girl. You're in good hands.' He returned his attention to Vaspine. 'Good luck cap'. Tell the old codger Cid's looking forward to having him back.'

Cid slapped the transporter's hull, then started to make his way back to the bridge. On the transporter, the captain checked a series of dials, adjusted a couple of knobs and tapped the throttle. The machine's engine whirred to life. Zoya felt a rumble as the craft jolted off the side of the *Dragonfly*, then a loud bang as its stabilizers kicked in. The next thing she knew, they were skipping through the sky like a stone on a lake.

44

For a while, neither Zoya nor the captain spoke. She watched the *Dragonfly* shrink behind them, until eventually it disappeared over the horizon. Vaspine followed the path of a river down the mountain, twisting and turning so as not to lose the stream beneath the canopy of the forest that clung to the rocks. In time, the river broadened, until Zoya realized they were flying over the opening of what had to be an enormous lake. She watched the body of water below as it drifted by.

After a few minutes, the patch of blue came to an abrupt halt ahead. Beyond, a monolithic, granite wall curved across the valley. Zoya peered at the wall, formed by cubes of rock as big as their transporter, and realized it was a dam. As they floated over the wall, Zoya loosened her safety belt and leaned over the edge of the transporter. The dam was huge. It had to be as wide as five *Dragonflys*, and just as tall. Zoya spotted a few other civilian transporters buzzing about the dam, and she thrust out an arm to wave, but Vaspine leaned across and pulled it down. 'Be careful,' he said. 'You never know who might be watching.'

The Doc's village was a seaside settlement situated where the plains of the great city of Dalmacia met the sea. As they neared the area, Zoya spotted huge, billowing plumes of smoke unfurling from the collection of buildings, expanding as they drifted into the sky. Vaspine's face grew increasingly severe the more he saw of the scene.

'What's wrong?'

Vaspine ignored Zoya and instead lowered the transporter, bringing it down beside a copse of trees outside the village. 'Have you got a weapon?' he asked as he catapulted out of his seat.

Zoya shook her head.

They walked cautiously to the outskirts of the village. With each step, the stench of fire and smoke grew, until Zoya started to retch. Vaspine tore off a strip of his shirt and motioned for Zoya to cover her mouth.

Eventually, they reached a low cliff that overlooked the ocean and village. From here, Zoya could see the place was decimated. Burnt-out buildings lined the streets, their faces blackened with soot. Nearby trees had burned too, stripped of their vegetation and standing like skeletons. Littering the roads were dozens of people, moving backwards and forwards like ants, their faces blank. Near to the ocean, a handful of houses still burned. Villagers nearby daisy-chained buckets of water, trying to put them out.

'What happened?' asked Zoya.

'I don't know,' said the captain. He lifted his spyglass to his eye. 'But it doesn't look good. Stay alert.'

A narrow, rocky path zigzagged down the cliff, before merging with another that crossed the beach to the village. Zoya and the captain took both of these, moving slowly, almost reluctant to reach their destination. Outside the settlement, they were met by a group of villagers. A man strode out of the group towards them, his face and hands blackened. 'We don't want any more of your type around here,' he said. 'Leave now, or I shan't be responsible for what happens.'

Vaspine glanced at Zoya, then back at the man. 'Our type? I was just hiking with my daughter when we saw the smoke.'

The old man shook his head. 'I spent twenty years in the Aviation Army, son. I know a sky thief when I see one.'

Vaspine dropped his smile. 'What happened?'

'Your kind, that's what happened.'

'What do you mean?'

'Sky thieves!' yelled a woman from the back of the crowd. 'Burned everything.'

Vaspine manoeuvred Zoya so she was behind him. 'Sky thieves? Why?'

'If I knew that I'd have stopped it,' said the old man.

'Who was it?' asked Vaspine.

The old man swiped a hand through the air to signify he'd had enough of the conversation, then turned away. The villagers started to follow him back to the village. Zoya looked up at Vaspine, waiting for him to speak. When he didn't, she stepped forward. 'Tall man. Moustache. Top hat.'

The old man froze. He continued to stare at the village.

'He's after us too,' continued Zoya, jabbing a thumb into her chest. 'We need to speak to someone inside your village about stopping him.'

For a moment, the old man looked like he was about to listen, then he shook his head. 'There's nothing left here. Be on your way.'

To Zoya's left, Vaspine stepped forward. 'Do you have an airship?'

The old man turned around. 'Don't see how it's any of your business, but one survived, yes.'

'Can you see that speck in the sky?' asked Vaspine, glancing over his shoulder.

Zoya looked up. Off in the distance, past the cliff-face and beyond Dalmacia's towering city wall, she spotted the captain's dot.

'That's my airship,' continued Vaspine. 'The *Dragonfly*. Send one of your people up. Tell my crew I sent you. Ask them to get some rations together. And some money.'

The old man furrowed his brow. 'The *Dragonfly*? I've heard of them.'

'We've got enough on board now for you to start rebuilding.' Vaspine nodded at the charred houses. 'And there'll be more later.'

The old man appealed to the crowd. A few wrinkled their noses, but most shrugged. 'Might as well,' said one. 'Can't get any worse.'

The old man considered Vaspine's proposition, then gestured for a young lad to approach. He whispered into the youngster's ear, then sent him back to town. 'Well,' he said, extending a hand, 'I guess you two had better come inside and tell me what you want.'

45

The old man led them into the village and through the streets to a walkway that overlooked the beach. They sat there with their legs overhanging the water. 'I'd have invited you into my house,' he said, 'but it's still on fire.'

Vaspine explained their reason for being there and offered the man one of the biscuits he'd brought from the *Dragonfly*. The old man took one, broke it in half and tossed the pieces to a pair of dogs sniffing at a nearby pile of trash. 'I know who you mean,' he said, cutting Vaspine off mid-sentence. 'Your fellow in the top hat was looking for him too.'

'Kane?'

'Is that who it was?' The old man spat in the water. 'I wish I'd never invited this Doc into town. He's brought us nothing but trouble.'

Vaspine nodded.

'That doesn't mean I'd give him up to any Dick and Harry,' said the old man. 'This Kane, he came with a bunch

180

of thugs, said he was looking for a scientist. I told him we don't have any, but he didn't listen, just burst through and started to rip open doors. A couple of our lads stood up to them, but, well . . .' He nodded down the walkway at two man-sized boxes resting against the wall. 'Let's just say he wasn't happy.

'The Doc's lab's underground. He's been surveying some fishes on the sea floor. Anagopas. He's built a viewing gallery. Thankfully, Kane didn't find the entrance and my people were brave enough to keep it secret. The Doc doesn't know how close he came to . . .' The old man trailed off as he tossed a stone into the water. The dogs barked at the noise. 'Not that it's helped us, mind. Look at what he's done.'

Zoya looked again at the town. It was like a warzone.

'We'll help,' said Vaspine.

'I'm sure you will. But that won't stop him doing it again, will it, to somewhere else?'

A silence descended as the three stared out to sea. Zoya glanced at the *Dragonfly*, still hovering up high. She hoped the boy would return soon.

'Anyhow,' said the man, groaning as he pushed himself up, 'don't take offence, but I'd rather get you two to this Doc right away. The sooner we get you out of the village, the safer people will feel.'

They followed the man through the streets, trying their best to avoid the gazes of the townspeople sitting outside their destroyed homes. He led them down the main thoroughfare that ran up from the beach, past the market square to a second walkway at the far end of town. When he arrived, he pointed to the beach. 'Under the pier. Keep walking for a few minutes and you'll come to a doorway. The Doc's lab's through there.'

With that, the old man nodded at the captain and trudged back to the market.

Zoya watched him go, then ran to catch up with Vaspine as he sidestepped down the wooden staircase from the walkway to the beach. 'Why did he do this?' she asked. 'Kane?'

'Because he's clever,' said Vaspine. 'He figured we'd try to get away, so he came to snatch the one person who could help us.'

Zoya looked back at the town. 'I hate him.'

'Good,' said Vaspine. 'Keep that in your head. And be alert. He might have left spies.'

The captain's warning stirred Zoya, and she continued to scan the beach for any movement. Eventually, they reached the doorway, an oak panel built into the frame of the pier. Vaspine poked around for a minute to make sure he knew the way out should they need it, then he pulled out the money pouch from his pocket and nodded at the door. 'Remember,' he said, patting Zoya on the back, 'we need him. Do whatever it takes.'

With that, he turned the door handle and pushed Zoya inside.

46

'He wants WHAT?' roared the Doc.

'He wants you to speed up the ship,' repeated Zoya, edging away.

'He wants it quicker?' shouted the Doc. 'With only one sail?'

Zoya shrugged.

'He's mad. The *Dragonfly*'s already the only ship out there with its own sun-ray processing unit. And now he comes down here, asking me to leave my beautiful fishes, to make the thing go *faster*? With one sail! What does he expect me to do? No, no, no, I might as well try to pull a bunch of flowers out of my ears.'

Zoya sighed. There were two things she could already tell about the scientist. The first was that if the Doc wasn't the most curious-looking man on the planet, then the fellow who beat him had to look something like an alien. Bright red hair that catapulted off his head, black-rimmed glasses with lenses so thick you could use them as dinner plates, a moustache as full as Zoya's hair, and eyes that seemed to bulge out of their sockets, all combined to make him look like an exceedingly eccentric man.

Secondly, the Doc had to be one of the world's untidiest men. From the moment she'd entered his lab, Zoya had felt like she was trying to navigate a hedge maze.

There were things *everywhere*.

It looked like the Doc had purchased every scientific instrument he'd ever seen, arranged for them all to be delivered to his lab, laid each item carefully on a shelf and then exploded a bomb. There were vials and test-tubes and measuring jugs in cupboards, on cupboards, on desks, and in smashed piles on the floor. There were square mechanical machines that chugged along, periodically emitting puffs of steam. There were clay models of fishes, skeletons made from beach shells, dead insects, and rotten vegetables. There were lamps and rulers and snapped pencils. Even the walls were covered, with chalkboards, diagrams, and blueprints.

Sauntering through all of this—sniffing at a skull here, licking a lantern there—was a cat with orange fur. Zoya first noticed the animal when it leapt out from behind a rotten pumpkin and aimed a swipe at her face. Years of orphanage food fights meant Zoya was quick enough to avoid the cat's claws, and it went sailing past and landed on top of one of the boxy machines. A puff of steam erupted below its backside, and it leapt onto a bookshelf. There, it curled into a ball and eyed Zoya warily.

'What's her name?' Zoya asked the Doc.

'*He*,' replied the Doc, 'is called Sol. Now, would you mind telling me who you are? Because I've not met you before and I don't normally let strangers into my lab—especially those who associate with that dagger-handling, skymap-breaking nincompoop.'

Zoya explained who she was and why Vaspine had sent her. This, in turn, led the Doc to storm around his lab as if someone had strapped a firework to his shoes. Finally, he came to a standstill near his desk, wiped an old sandwich off his chair and plonked himself down. He stared at Zoya again, unable to believe she was Jupiter and Dominika's daughter. 'Really?' He shook his head, then pointed to a small metal box in the opposite corner of the room. 'Do you see that machine?'

Zoya nodded.

'You've got one on the *Dragonfly*. It's called a sun-ray processor. Unless someone's worked out how to make one, this and the one on your ship are the only two in existence. That means the *Dragonfly* is the only airship able to propel itself with sunlight alone. If you didn't need food, you'd never have to land at all.'

'Impressive,' said Zoya.

The Doc watched Zoya to see if she was mocking him. 'The problem,' he said, 'is that solar power isn't anywhere near as efficient as oil. So when you go up against a *good* oil engine, like the *Shadow*'s Injektor, you struggle. The *Dragonfly*'s quick, but the *Shadow*'s quicker.'

Zoya ran her hand along the top of the processor. 'How does it work?'

The Doc chortled. 'If it was that easy, I wouldn't have spent ten years studying at the University of Dalmacia.'

'Try me,' said Zoya.

47

The Doc sighed, then walked to his machine. 'You see the tubes coming out the back?'

'Yes.'

'You've got the same on the *Dragonfly*. They lead all the way up to the deck. You might have missed them, they're disguised as rigging. There are around a dozen that come out of the back of the machine, each one a different rope on the surface. Clever, eh?'

'I guess,' said Zoya.

The Doc rolled his eyes. 'She guesses! Anyway, up on deck, these tubes run up the mainmast and fan out into the framework of the sails. Do you know where I mean?'

Zoya thought of the times she and Bucker had scaled the ropes on their way to the lookout pod and nodded.

'Well, those aren't actually sails, they're giant solar collectors. Dotted across them are tiny indentations, into which pools solar energy. This energy is fed into tubes, which run down below deck and into this chamber.'

The Doc bent and unlatched the door of the chamber, revealing a floating, incandescent globe. 'This, miss, is the reason your captain's request is so absurd, and why it would be nigh on impossible to get double the power from a single sail, even if I were to consider it,' he added quickly, 'which I'm not! This is a mini-sun—a smaller version of the real one. It gets fed all the energy your solar sails collect and uses it to power your airship.'

Zoya whistled.

'But there's a snag,' continued the Doc. 'These mini-suns are already as big as they can be. If you get rid of a sail, you need to increase the size of the mini-sun. But any bigger and they might start generating their own gravity and suck everything in. That includes you, me, Kane, and the good captain.'

'So let's make a second,' said Zoya.

'Hmphh!' The Doc scoffed. 'If it were that easy, I'd be a millionaire. This is a mini-*sun*. They don't grow on trees. All that energy . . .' the Doc stared into the distance, '. . . you have to give something priceless. The two I've made were catalyzed by crystals.' He looked at the glowing globe in the chamber. 'This one by a Xana. The one on the *Dragonfly* by an Algrond.'

Zoya's face brightened. 'So we can take this one?'

The Doc shook his head. 'You can't *move* the things. Once they're set, that's where they stay.'

'So there's nothing we can do?' asked Zoya.

'I didn't say that,' said the Doc, closing the chamber and chomping on the sandwich he'd moved earlier. 'Just that it wasn't a good idea.'

'So there is something?'

'There's always something.' The Doc laid the remains of his sandwich before Sol and walked to his laboratory door. 'But that's for you and the captain to work out.' He swung an arm for her to leave. 'I liked your parents, Zoya. But anyone on the *Dragonfly* will tell you I'm not known for helping people. The last thing I'm going to do is go up against Kane. Goodbye.'

On her way in, the captain had told Zoya to offer the Doc the money only as a last resort ('food's running a bit short, and we don't know what else we'll need over the next few days. Hold onto it if you can,'), but Zoya was starting to think it might be time. 'OK,' she said, getting up. 'If you don't want to help, I guess that's fine.'

The Doc smiled. 'I know.'

Zoya crossed to the door. As she went, she scooped up the money bag from where she'd left it on the desk. 'It's a shame. We could do with the help.'

'Jolly good,' said the Doc.

Zoya sighed. 'Oh well, looks like we'll have to find somebody else to give these hundred coins to . . .'

'That's fine,' said the Doc. 'I'm sure they'll appreciate the opportun—' He paused. 'How much?'

189

Zoya glanced at the bag. 'A hundred. But that wouldn't interest a genius like you.' She approached the door, watching the Doc through the corner of her eye. A battle raged on his face, one that shifted from confusion to irritation to lust. Eventually, he wrung his hands. 'Now, hang on . . .'

'No,' said Zoya. 'I can see I'm disturbing you.'

'Hold on.' The Doc laughed nervously. 'I didn't know there was such a . . .' he paused, reaching for the bag, '. . . handsome sum on the line. I didn't say I couldn't help. In fact . . .' the Doc stepped to the blackboard. He scribbled on it with a piece of chalk——small, spidery figures that Zoya struggled to read, let alone understand. For three minutes he scratched, sighing periodically and then looking to the heavens for inspiration. Zoya's leg started to ache and she searched for a place to sit. Noticing a plate of mouldy food on the desk, she picked it up to put it in the bin. Without turning, the Doc shouted. 'Don't touch that!'

'But it's gone off,' said Zoya.

'That's the point.'

After another round of doodling, he finally turned and pointed at his work. 'That might do it.'

'What?' asked Zoya.

'Goodness!' The Doc threw up his hands. 'Did the captain send his most dim-witted monkey? Watch. If I load double the amount of solar rays into the machine, constrain it using Helios's Law,' he swept his hand across the blackboard, revealing what had to be the world's longest mathematical equation, 'then I should,' the Doc repeated the word, '*should*, be able to get the same amount of power from one sail.'

Zoya grinned. 'That's great. What shall I tell the captain?'

The Doc rolled his eyes. 'Tell that crazy nincompoop I'll come back.'

48

While Zoya had been inside speaking to the Doc, Vaspine had arranged for one of the townspeople to grab their transporter from where he'd left it. He gave the Doc five minutes to gather his belongings and anything he'd need to fix the *Dragonfly* ('you're joking, I couldn't pack a satchel in five minutes!'). After he lifted his final box into the transporter, the Doc leapt back to the beach, darted into his lab and emerged once more with Sol under his arm. Juggling the scratching, squirming cat, he took a key and locked the door. 'Don't worry,' said the captain, 'you'll be back. If you get us away from Kane, I guarantee I'll never come knocking again.'

'That's what you said last time.'

The journey back to the *Dragonfly* was quiet. Zoya spotted the craft first, a dot on the horizon hovering between the tips of two peaks. Beyond, the sky had darkened to a roiling, bubbling mass of greys and indigos. The trio were greeted on board by Rosie and Cid, who helped ease the transporter back into the space at the ship's bow. Vaspine flicked off the engine and climbed out. Rosie moved forward to help the Doc, while Cid rounded the back of the transporter and started to transfer his boxes to the deck.

'Be careful with those,' snapped the Doc. 'Those instruments are worth hundreds of coins.'

'Nice to see you too,' said Cid.

'I'm only here to get you numbskulls out of another mess, then I'm gone. I presume my old lab's intact?' He addressed this to Vaspine.

'It's all yours. Doc, you've got an hour. After that, meet in my quarters with a plan.'

'Yeah yeah,' said the Doc. He bent to retrieve Sol from the transporter and staggered off down the deck.

'I can see he hasn't changed,' said Rosie, when he was out of earshot.

'Is he always like that?' asked Zoya.

'On good days,' said Cid.

The captain crossed to the side of the ship and took in a lungful of air. 'Anything to report?'

'Nothing,' said Cid.

'No sign of . . .'

'No.'

Vaspine nodded. 'OK.' He rubbed his eyes. 'I'm going to my cabin. Rosie, come with me. We need to have a think about what we're going to do after the Dalmacia Pass. Cid,

Zoya, get these boxes down to the Doc and give him anything else he needs. We'll meet in my quarters in an hour.'

Zoya and Cid did as instructed, trudging between the laboratory and the transporter three times before the craft was empty. When they'd finished, the sun was starting to set behind what remained of the solar sails. The Doc stood in their shadow, Sol perched on his shoulder and a spyglass to his eye. In his right hand he balanced a notebook.

'Think he'll be able to do it?' asked Bucker, approaching to Zoya's left.

Zoya thought a moment. 'You got any more of those cards under the table?'

49

A conference was already underway when Zoya arrived at the captain's quarters. Beebee was there, locked in a heated conversation with the captain, who sat with his feet up on his desk. Rosie and Cid were there too, holding their own discussion by the skymap. They all fell silent when they noticed Zoya. She took a seat on the arm of the sofa and looked at the captain.

'Well,' said Vaspine, 'guess we're just waiting for the Doc.'

As if on cue, the scientist stumbled through the door, his hair even more bedraggled than usual and his cheeks red. In his right hand he swung the notebook Zoya had seen him with earlier, and in the crook of his left arm he carried a glass-panelled, blackened box. A crack marred one of the cube's faces, opening to a fist-sized hole. The Doc deposited the cube on one of the captain's bookcases and turned to face the others. For a moment, he considered what to say, then walked to a nearby shelf and pulled down a wooden model of the *Dragonfly*. He held it up for everyone to see, then

195

pulled off the sails and snapped them in half. 'These are your sails,' he said.

'Steady,' said Cid, rising from his seat. 'She's hurt, but she can still fly.'

'She might stay in the air,' said the Doc. 'But she's a dead duck when it comes to outrunning Kane.'

'Enough!' snapped Vaspine. He eyeballed the Doc. 'You said you can speed us up using one sail. I presume you still can?'

The Doc approached the blackened cube, gathered it up, walked to the captain's dining table and deposited it there, its cracked face towards them. 'The damage is worse than you thought,' he said, addressing the captain. 'A few of the meteorites made it down to the engine room.'

'Is that the . . .?'

The Doc nodded. 'One of them hit the mini-sun. It's gone.'

'Gone?' said Rosie. She shook her head. 'So restart it.'

The Doc glanced at the captain, who'd turned from the others and was leaning on his fists on his desk. 'We can't,' said the Doc, eventually.

'Why?'

'Once it's out, you can't start a new one without a catalyst.'

'So we'll get one,' said Cid.

Vaspine lifted his head. 'It's not going to happen. It's over.'

'What do you mean, it's over?' said Cid. 'It's not over.'

'What do you suggest then?' said Vaspine. 'We've got no power. We can't run. There's no way we'd make it to the Dalmacia Pass without Kane finding us first.'

'We fight,' said Beebee.

Vaspine raised a palm.

'I'm just saying . . .'

'Enough.' The captain's voice was sharp. 'It's not that simple. You might be confident we can win against the *Shadow*, but I've got a bunch of people on this ship who'd disagree.' Vaspine paused to calm himself. 'Cid?'

The pilot stroked his moustache. 'Captain, I can't tell you how much I want to take down Kane.' He paused, choosing his words. 'But you're right. If we go after that ship today, we die.'

Vaspine inhaled once, then walked to his skymap and slammed his fist onto the surface. Zoya jumped at the captain's outburst, then scanned the map for the *Dragonfly*'s current location. She made out the towering city of Dalmacia, as well as the Dalmacian mountain range stretching to the north.

'Ideas,' said the captain. 'I need ideas.'

The room swirled with a tornado of opinions. Zoya watched the adults, their voices seeming far away. She found herself drawn to the skymap. Something caught her attention. Floating just above the surface, not far from Dalmacia, was a dark lump of rock. An image formed in her mind, a shining yellow light. 'Stop!' she shouted.

The adults silenced.

'I know what to do.' Zoya turned to the Doc. 'Doc, is what you said back at your lab true? About the Algrond Crystal?'

Before the Doc could answer, Vaspine shot a look at Zoya. 'Zoya, that's just a rumour . . .'

'Yes or no?' Zoya asked the Doc.

The Doc swung his head towards Vaspine, who nodded for him to answer. 'Yes. It's true.' He laughed, throwing his head back. 'But that's like asking for a miracle. There are four in the world, for lord's sake.'

Zoya pointed towards the floating rock on the skymap. 'And captain, you told me before this was the Island in the Sky?'

'Yes.'

Zoya jumped up from the arm of the sofa and rounded the skymap. 'How far away are we, Cid?'

The pilot glanced at the map and shrugged. 'If the ship moves like she did today? Half a day.'

'What's at the Island in the Sky that could help?' asked Zoya. The adults glanced at Vaspine, who folded his arms and dipped his head in Zoya's direction. The others continued to think, then looked amongst each other. None could work it out. Zoya threw up her hands. 'The vault!'

One by one, grins started to spread across their faces. 'We go there,' said Zoya. 'If the rumours are true, there's an Algrond Crystal inside. We bring it back, the Doc starts a new mini-sun and we make it through the Dalmacia Pass.'

'Zoya,' said Cid, shaking his head. 'You little genius.'

'I know.'

'That may be so,' said Vaspine, stepping forwards. 'But it's risky. *If* the crystal's inside—and it's a big if—there are thieves all over the island. And the vault's a pig to reach. We wouldn't be able to get the ship in close. Nor a transporter. We'd have to walk.'

Zoya shrugged. 'You guys would help, right?'

Rosie smiled. 'Of course.'

'Then I'll be fine.'

One by one, the adults' faces lit up. Eventually, an impatient Cid clapped his hands. 'So, Doc, how about it? If we get you a crystal, can you get this thing moving again?'

The Doc shook his head, trying to hold in what he was about to say. 'Yes,' he blurted, eventually, growing more enthusiastic by the second. 'Yes! If you get me the crystal, I'll get you flying!'

Cid smiled. 'Well,' he said, slapping his hands to his thighs and pushing himself to his feet, 'we can't just sit around here all day congratulating ourselves on a good idea. Some of us have to fly this hunk of junk. So, the Island in the Sky?'

They all looked at the captain. He nodded.

50

Cid used the skymap to plan a journey between the *Dragonfly* and the Island in the Sky, avoiding known routes wherever possible, as well as Aviation Army airbases and any one of a hundred other things that could expose them to Kane. He came up with a time of fifteen hours. 'Best I can do,' he said.

Later that evening, Vaspine informed the rest of the crew. There were some grumbles of dissent, but for the most part they agreed with the captain's decision. 'We're damned if we fight,' snarled Maddie, 'and damned if we run. Might as well at least *try*.'

Zoya slept little that night. In the morning, she slipped through the fog, slaloming through the walkways towards the rear of the ship. Unhooking the hatch Charlie had shown her a couple of days before, she clambered down to the lower decks. From the foot of the ladder, she made her way to the gym. Rosie was already there, arranging hoops on the floor. 'You caught my wink last night then?'

Zoya nodded.

'The captain would want you out on deck preparing, but I think we've got a bit more preparing of our own to do.' Rosie nodded at Zoya's stomach. 'Have you eaten?'

She shook her head.

'Good. I don't want to be cleaning up any sick!'

Rosie started her off with ten minutes of jumping jacks, followed by ten minutes of leaping onto and off a foot-high bench. When Zoya's legs started to wobble, they transitioned to a new circuit of five exercises: push-ups, pull-ups, sit-ups, squats, and lunges. Positioning a five-minute hourglass on the bench so Zoya could see it draining, Rosie challenged her to perform twenty of each before the timer ran out. It was after just a third of this time that Zoya stumbled backwards off the bench and sank to the floor.

'That took longer than I expected,' she said. 'Most people don't make it onto the second bit.'

After a two-minute break, during which Rosie allowed Zoya a sip of water, she ordered her back to her feet. This time, she alternated more exercises with sessions of sword-fighting skills. The work was much harder than before, and Zoya soon realized Rosie had gone easy on her the first time. She started to feel a little out of her depth.

Still, Zoya persevered. And two long hours after starting, Rosie flung her sword aside and called the workout to an end. Zoya was so shattered she could barely lift herself off the floor. Rosie tidied the gym around her as Zoya caught her breath. 'Tired?'

Zoya nodded.

'You know how I can tell when people are really tired?' asked Rosie. 'They get this look in their eyes that tells me they want to kill me.'

Zoya tried to laugh, but all that came out was a cough.

'Come here,' said Rosie. She walked over, placed her arms under Zoya and hauled her up. Rosie walked to her bench, took her hand, put it to her own chest and breathed slowly and deeply. 'Try to follow my breathing.'

Zoya did. After a few seconds, she noticed her own start to slow.

'You know,' said Rosie, removing her hand. 'I was planning to teach you one last thing today, but I think it should wait.'

Zoya looked up. 'What?'

'Nothing,' said Rosie. 'You're exhausted.'

Zoya drew herself up. 'I'm not. Tell me.'

Rosie eyed her. 'Are you sure. Because this isn't easy. This kind of thing can get you hurt if you're not ready.'

'I'm ready,' said Zoya.

Rosie thought for a moment, then sighed. 'OK. Grab that ring from the ceiling.'

Zoya climbed onto a bench, positioned herself beneath the hoop and jumped as high as she could. The ring came away in her hand and dangled on a length of rope a foot above her head. Rosie instructed her to do the same with three more — one near the first, and two at the other side of the room. Satisfied, Rosie gripped one end of their training bench and motioned for Zoya to grab the other. Together, they hoisted it above their heads and slotted it between the pairs of rings so that it hung above them. Rosie grabbed the bench and pulled herself up. 'Chuck me that sword.'

Zoya grabbed the weapon and threw it up.

'Now,' said Rosie. 'I've taught you the most important rule in fighting, which is?'

'Always get the higher ground,' repeated Zoya for the tenth time that day.

'If you're fighting someone and they've got the higher ground, move so you take it from them. It's that simple. Because without it you'll lose.' Rosie shifted nimbly. 'However,' she pointed her sword at Zoya, 'sometimes you can't get the higher ground. What do you do then?'

Zoya shrugged. 'Run?'

Rosie laughed. 'No, if you can't get to the higher ground and you can't move to the side, your only option is . . .'

'Down,' finished Zoya.

'Precisely. Watch.'

Rosie adopted her fighting stance. Without a word, she stepped off the side of the bench and dropped towards the floor. As she fell, she grabbed the edge of the platform with her left hand and swung underneath it in a loop. As her weight shifted from her left side to her right, she started to climb again, the momentum of her swing propelling her up. She landed back on the bench in a feline crouch, her sword pointing at Zoya.

Down below, Zoya's mouth hung open. The manoeuvre had taken no time at all. Had she blinked, she'd have missed it. And yet, it had happened. Rosie really had circled the bench in less than a second.

Zoya spluttered. 'Teach me . . .'

51

Rosie spent the next hour showing Zoya the move, drilling it over and over so Zoya would remember it like she remembered her name. When they were finished, she smiled as Zoya lay in a heap on the floor. 'I think that really will do for now.' Rosie wiped her hands on a towel. 'We're going to be at the Island in the Sky soon. You need to get ready.'

Feeling queasy, Zoya stumbled back to her cabin, cleaned up and collapsed on her bed. She stayed still for a while, trying to calm her dizzy mind. Reaching into her shirt, she pulled out her locket and cupped it in her hands. Briefly, she felt an urge to escape again, to go somewhere nobody knew her, somewhere she could eat and sleep in peace. It seemed like a dream.

And yet, there was something to admire about the sky thieves. The danger, the risk, the vast, endless skies, the meteorites and volcanoes and all the others things she'd never have experienced on the surface. The life ran in her veins. Jupiter and Dominika . . . she was their daughter. And now Bucker, Rosie, Beebee, Cid, the captain—she wanted to see the world with them. She wanted to raid cruisers, help burning villages . . .

She couldn't let Kane take that away.

Zoya was back out on the bridge when one of Cid's deputies first put out the call that the Island in the Sky was visible in the distance. She'd heard stories about the rock from people on the ship, but none had prepared her for what she saw when she poked her head over the gunwale. Floating in the sky, a dozen miles ahead, was a slab of rock so big it swallowed the entire horizon. Its underside—burnt umber in colour—was topped with a fringe of green forests and meadows. Rising from this, a chain of imposing mountains with snowy peaks gleamed purple in the sunlight. Nestled amongst the green below were glimpses of buildings.

'Amazing, isn't it?' Beebee said from further down the gunwale.

'It's . . .' Zoya trailed off.

'Strange?' said Beebee. 'You look and you look, and you think you're going to find the trick of how they keep it afloat, but you never do.'

'How *do* they?'

'No one knows.' said Beebee. 'It was making its way around long before people arrived, and it'll be making its way long after we're gone.'

'Is it going anywhere in particular?'

'Doesn't seem to be. Some of the innkeepers tried to record where it went for a few months, to make stock deliveries easier. There was no pattern. It just seems to go wherever it wants.'

The closer they drew, the more of the island Zoya wanted to see. Beebee noticed her struggling on her tiptoes to see over the side and hoisted her onto his shoulders.

The airship traffic around the island was dense, and Zoya felt sure they'd crash into something. Cid did his best to pilot them through. 'You always bang into one or two,' he said with a wink. 'Luckily, no one seems to mind.' The ship approached the island from the south, speeding over farmland and forests and colourful meadows occupied by galloping horses and snoozing sheep. It only started to slow when it reached a lake in the island's centre. Bobbing up and down on the water were dozens of boats.

'What's that?' asked Zoya.

At the lake's northern shore stood a cluster of buildings and roads. The structures were small, Zoya noted—none higher than three stories, dwarfs next to the soaring towers she'd seen in Dalmacia. But they were solid, and looked as though they'd been on the island for years.

'That's Moonfall,' said Beebee. 'Where all the thieves spend their stolen money. Inns, shops, saloons . . . If there's one place you don't want to be, it's there.'

They left the town behind and continued north up the island. Soon, the roads and buildings gave way to more fields, these wilder than those in the south. Ahead reared the mountain range Zoya had seen earlier. From Beebee's shoulder, the foothills of the mountains were easy to see, blanketed in dense forest. Cid aimed the ship at a large clearing just short of the trees and brought it down. As he flicked off the engine, he winked at Zoya. 'That's me done. The rest's up to you.'

52

Zoya returned to the central deck to find Vaspine already stuffing three knapsacks with blankets, tents, firewood, food, and water. Rosie followed him as he worked.

'Only three?' she said.

'Three's all we need.'

'Why not take some of my swordsmen? The more hands the better.'

Vaspine stopped what he was doing. 'Rosie, the more people we take, the more equipment we need, the more noise we make and the more likely we are to be noticed. If Kane has spies out there, we need to be discreet. That means three.'

The captain returned to his packing, but Rosie put a hand on his shoulder. 'Then let me go. You know I'm better with a sword. If Kane tries to attack, I'll protect her.'

'You've got your own lad to worry about,' said Vaspine.

'Bucker will be safe here. You and Cid can keep an eye on him.'

'No, *you* and Cid will keep an eye on him,' said Vaspine. 'Besides, I'm taking Beebee. Between us, we'll be able to handle things.'

'What if you can't?'

Vaspine thought. 'If I can't, then I want the *Dragonfly* out of here. In which case, I need someone on board who knows how to run the damn thing.' He nodded at Cid, then at Rosie. 'Cid flies, you're captain.'

'But . . .'

'No buts. I don't have time for this, Rosie. Go and give the crew some jobs to do while we're grounded. Keep them busy. Thank you.'

Rosie glared at the captain, then shook her head and walked away. She stopped when she realized Zoya had been listening. She laid a hand on the girl's shoulder. 'You'll be fine,' she said, and walked off towards the bow.

Zoya made her way to the captain and started to hand him things to put in the knapsacks. 'How long until we set off?'

'A few minutes,' said Vaspine. 'It's a day's walk up and down the mountain. We need to make sure we've got everything.'

Zoya stuffed another blanket into a bag. 'Will I need Storm?'

'Storm?'

'My sword.'

Vaspine closed his eyes, then opened them. 'Bring it.'

Zoya went quiet at this. She'd thought the journey to the vault would be straightforward. But seeing Rosie and the captain argue, she was no longer sure. 'Is what we're doing dangerous?'

'The whole island's dangerous,' said the captain. 'It's full of the foulest, most despicable liars, cheats, gamblers, and murderers. Most stick to Moonfall, but there'll be some up in the mountains. None of them know about your locket, but they might attack us anyway.' He looked at the sun, low in the sky. 'But there'll be nothing we can't handle. Clear?'

Zoya nodded.

'We'll spend the rest of today walking, camp, then another couple of hours walking, open the vault, return to the ship, the Doc can use the crystal and then we're gone, through the Dalmacia Pass and off to somewhere Kane can't find us. All you need to do in the meantime is stay close.'

'I'll try,' said Zoya.

'That's all anyone can do,' said Vaspine.

53

Most of the thieves on board stood at the port side to wave them goodbye. The trio marched in line away from the ship—the captain leading and Beebee bringing up the rear. Within five minutes, they'd disappeared around the corner from the *Dragonfly* and entered the dense forest Zoya had seen from the airship. They walked silently in the gloom, before coming across a path. 'This is what I was looking for,' said the captain. 'It should take us through the woods to the foot of the mountain.'

They followed the path for a couple of hours as it wound through the trees. As the day wore on, the light around them grew dimmer, until Zoya had to watch her footing to avoid tripping over sprawling roots and felled trunks.

There was a tension between Beebee and the captain. They avoided speaking the entire time they were on the trail, save to confirm their location or discuss strategies for navigating difficult terrain. Zoya had an idea what was wrong, but didn't get a chance to ask until the captain was caught short and had to wander into the trees. As soon as he was gone, she joined Beebee on the stump he'd chosen for a seat. 'You don't think this is a good idea, do you?'

Beebee shook his head.

'Don't you think we'll be able to get into the vault?'

'Probably. But we shouldn't be going near the place. It's a flawed plan. I've been a fighter since I was five—streets, boxing rings, airships. The one thing I've learned is that you never, ever run.'

Zoya shifted on the log.

'They always catch you,' he continued. 'The captain thinks we'll be in a better position to fight once we're on the other side of the Dalmacia Pass. We won't. We'll be in exactly the same position we're in now, except we'll be exhausted from trying to hide. The only way we're going to stop Kane is if we attack when he's not expecting it. That means now.' Beebee hurled a stone against a nearby tree trunk. He spoke his next words through gritted teeth. 'No, I don't think we should be going.'

Zoya remained silent. Beebee realized he'd upset her and laid a hand on her shoulder. 'I'm sorry,' he said. 'It's not as bad as I'm making out. We'll be fine. I just think we should have attacked. Maybe that's the boxer in me.' He laughed.

Shortly after, Vaspine emerged from the forest and shouldered his pack. 'Everyone OK?'

Zoya nodded.

When they eventually emerged from the wood, it was to a view that made her gasp. Silhouetted against the moon was a range of mountains that made the Dalmacians look like sand dunes. The mountains stretched across the horizon as far as Zoya could see—giant, craggy peaks with misty crowns. The path they'd taken through the forest continued into the hills. Zoya followed it with her binoculars, first up a gentle slope, then accelerating and out of sight. The slopes themselves were covered in shrubs—mere outlines in the dark—and here and there a few grazing animals nibbling on the grass.

'Is the vault up there?' she asked.

'Not all the way,' said Vaspine. 'It's buried in a valley just beyond that ridge.' He pointed to an outcrop halfway up. 'We'll make it to the point where the path bends around the mountain tonight. The rest of the journey will have to wait until morning.'

Vaspine looked at her. 'You're about to get a lot colder than you've ever been. Get any spare clothes you have and put them on. Now.'

They walked for two more hours in silence. Zoya's hearing sharpened, so that after a while she could hear the faraway howl of wolves as if they were nearby. At one point, she even thought she heard footsteps rustling behind them, but she didn't say anything and she didn't hear them again.

When they finally stopped, Zoya set up her tent on an

outcrop just off the main path that allowed her to look back on their journey. Way off in the distance she could see the twinkling lights of Moonfall, then closer the darkness of the forest. With the ground so solid beneath her, she had to remind herself they were on an island floating thousands of feet high.

Zoya found a thick blanket in her backpack and wrapped it around her shoulders. Vaspine and Beebee ghosted around, starting a fire and cooking some pork. All three were exhausted to the point of collapse, and they barely said a word for the rest of the evening. They ate, huddled around the campfire, and tried to draw warmth from its embers.

54

The captain was already awake when Zoya surfaced in the morning, stirring ashes with his walking stick. When he saw Zoya, he put down the stick and tossed her some bread. 'Sleep OK?'

'As well as you can when it feels like you're on ice.' Zoya squinted in the sunlight and scrubbed a patch of gravel with her boots.

'You think this is bad? I remember the first few years with your father. He'd bring us here without any tents and we'd sleep under the stars. *That* was icy.'

Vaspine pushed himself up and made his way to Beebee's tent. He shook the fabric, disturbing a pool of water that had collected overnight. 'Besides,' said Vaspine, 'it wouldn't be sky thieving if there wasn't a bit of a challenge.'

Beebee had slept well, and he woke in a better mood than the day before. Vaspine passed around the few scraps of meat left from their evening meal. On any other day, the leftovers would have made a poor excuse for breakfast, but that morning they tasted like a feast.

Once they'd eaten, they packed up their tents, shouldered their backpacks and spent a few minutes scuffing up their camp so it looked like they'd never been there. 'Can't be too careful,' said Beebee.

Vaspine had said Jupiter's vault wasn't far, so in spite of aching legs Zoya didn't feel too bad when they resumed walking. Ahead, the path rounded the side of the mountain and narrowed to a ridge flanked either side by steep drops. As the morning wore on, the weather started to deteriorate. A fog rolled in across the valley, growing thicker the higher they climbed. After an hour, it was so misty Zoya could no longer be sure her next step would land on solid rock.

Vaspine decided to stop until it passed. They huddled together in the middle of the path and shivered for an hour before Vaspine realized things were unlikely to improve. 'We can go back,' he said, 'or we can continue. But we can't stay.'

Zoya glanced back down the mountain. The thought of having to climb it again later made her stomach churn. 'Let's push on.'

Beebee nodded in agreement.

Before starting up again, Vaspine retrieved a length of rope from his backpack and attached it to Beebee's waist, then Zoya's, and finally his own. 'This should keep us together.'

Beebee chuckled. 'If one falls, we all fall.'

The trio fought the fog for another hour before Zoya noticed the path turn a corner ahead. 'Good,' said the captain, 'we're nearly there.'

Around the bend, the trail spilled onto a huge slab of rock that jutted out from the side of the mountain. The rest of the peak soared behind it. In the shade of the great wall, the weather was less severe. There were still a few lingering wisps of fog, but otherwise the air was calm.

Zoya dumped her pack on the ground and looked around. She was surprised to see the path vanish where it met the cliff. She rubbed her eyes and blinked to check she wasn't imagining things. 'Why would someone make a path that leads into a cliff?' she asked the captain.

'Why indeed?' agreed Vaspine. He jogged ahead, laid his hands on the rock and turned to face Zoya and Beebee. 'Did you ever hear the one about the vanishing captain?'

'Nope,' said Zoya.

'Now you see him,' Vaspine took a short hop to his left, 'now you don't.'

It took Zoya a moment to realize the captain had gone. When she did, her brain nearly imploded. She exchanged a glance with Beebee, whose face registered the same amazement, before they each ran to the cliff to investigate. They searched all around the point of the captain's disappearance, but there was no sign of him. Zoya shrugged.

'You'll have to do better than that,' said Vaspine's voice.

Zoya spun around and walked to where she thought it had originated. 'Closer,' said Vaspine. Zoya walked backwards and forwards past the spot, but couldn't see anything. Then, something on the rock-face caught her eye. What had looked like a single crag was actually two, angled together to look like one. Zoya ran over, and sure enough there was a gap wide enough to fit a man. She reached inside and there, chuckling, was the captain.

Vaspine wriggled out of the gap. 'Neat, eh?'

'Amazing,' said Beebee. 'Is that the vault?'

The captain shook his head. 'No, but it's how Jupiter kept it hidden from the greedy hands on this island.' He slid back through the gap. 'Come and see.'

55

Zoya followed first, shimmying in sideways. Beebee edged in after, lifting his backpack above his head to squeeze through. The crack soon widened, allowing them to walk forwards. Zoya heard the echo of Vaspine's footsteps, although she couldn't see the captain. 'Not much further,' she heard him say.

The tunnel grew so dark that they could barely see. Rivulets of water trickled down the wall, deafening in the enclosed space. A little further on, Zoya noticed a strip of light ahead. In the centre was the captain's silhouette. When Zoya reached the opening she had to stop to take in the view. They'd arrived at the mouth of a lush green valley. Gone were the barren fields and dull stretches of land, replaced by two steep cliffs either side of a grassy central plain. Dispersed along it were towering rock formations covered in fuzzy green moss, tumbling waterfalls, copses of trees, flowers of every shape and colour, and a small lake.

'How does this even exist?' asked Zoya.

'It's a sheltered valley,' explained Vaspine. 'The high walls mean it has its own climate. The cold air can't get here, and the sun runs in a direct line overhead. Add a little rain and you've got a paradise.'

'Where's the vault?' asked Beebee.

Vaspine pointed to the valley's eastern wall, to a spot halfway along. Nestled in the cliff was a white circle, reachable only—as far as Zoya could tell—by a staircase carved into the rock below. Zoya estimated the circle to be as wide as three people. She trained her binoculars on the shape and realized it was the vault's door. Its rivets were as big as Zoya's head and seemed to be made from the same dark metal as her locket, only appearing white in the sun.

'Let's go,' said Zoya.

They followed the path onto the plains, then cut across the meadow and made their way up the staircase. The door was bigger than Zoya had estimated, perhaps the width of five men. 'Must be huge inside.'

They shook off their backpacks, then Vaspine and Beebee stood aside and gestured for Zoya to approach.

'What do I do?'

'Try the locket,' said Vaspine.

Zoya pulled out the pendant and unclipped it from her neck. She felt it vibrate in her palm. And it had changed colour from its usual dark tone to a soft, pulsing blue.

'That's a good start,' said Vaspine.

Zoya walked towards the door. With each stride, the locket grew brighter until it was glowing. With five paces to go, its juddering became violent, and it emitted a thunderous drone that made her want to throw her hands to her ears. Each step caused the sensation to intensify, until it was difficult for Zoya to hold on. 'I'm going to drop it!'

'You won't,' said Vaspine.

Zoya tightened her grip. She took another step forwards, and again the vibration intensified. At this point, she realized the locket wasn't so much vibrating as being pulled towards the door. She took another step—she was close now—and yet again the reverberation increased. Without waiting, she thrust the locket out so that it made contact with the door. As soon as the pendant touched the metal, there was a loud *whoosh*, and the door slid across until it rested against the rock to Zoya's right. Before her was an opening. Vaspine and Beebee raced up behind her and peered inside.

The vault was as large as the *Dragonfly*'s deck, its walls carved in a perfect oblong and smooth like porcelain. A procession of plinths lined the sides, as high as Zoya. On each rested an ornate wooden chest, their lids open to reveal mounds of jewellery and gold. Zoya walked into the room, spinning as she did to take in the view. She approached the nearest chest, lifted a handful of coins and let them trickle back to the pile. 'Oh my God,' she said, turning to the others.

Vaspine smiled.

'There has to be . . .' Zoya looked around, '. . . thousands here.'

'At least,' said the captain.

'Where's the crystal?'

Vaspine shrugged. 'We'll have to look.'

Zoya shook her head, bemused that her father would discard something so precious amongst the other trinkets. Vaspine and Beebee joined her in searching, sifting through the coins and jewellery, unsure what they were looking for but hoping they'd know when they found it. At one point, in a chest near the far end of the vault, Zoya fingered a smooth, blue crystal, which sent a buzz of excitement through her. She pulled this out eagerly, sweeping away the gold coins as if they were pebbles, but was disappointed to find the orb attached to a silver tiara.

'Why did he keep so much *money*?' she asked the captain. 'Why didn't he give it away?'

Vaspine crossed to a new chest and lifted a chunky gold ring from the pile there. He tried it on his finger. 'Insurance. Sky thieving's dangerous. Your father wanted this in case he needed to start again.'

Zoya pinched her lips. 'And this is what Kane wants? He killed my parents for *this*?'

'This and the crystal,' said Vaspine.

Zoya eventually found the Algrond Crystal wedged into the side of a chest, buried beneath a gold magnifying glass and a silver compass. Zoya dislodged the gem carefully and held it up to the stream of light. It had to be the one. 'Got it!'

The crystal was slightly larger than her hand—a heavy, misshapen amber lump, longer on one axis, so that it looked like a potato. Its sides were banded, and half-gleaming half-dull, depending on where Zoya looked and how it caught the wedge of light streaming in through the door. The captain and Beebee came up behind her and leaned in to see for themselves. The captain nodded. 'Bang on.' He ran a finger along the edge of the crystal. A fine powder settled on his fingertip. 'I really don't think your father knew the true value of this thing.'

'No,' said Zoya, glancing back at the chest. 'Neither do I.'

Zoya looked at Beebee. He didn't speak, but he was smiling too. When he saw her, he winked. 'Let's load the bags and scram before it gets dark.'

56

They dumped from their packs everything they were unlikely to need for the return journey and loaded them with gold. Zoya placed the Algrond Crystal in a pocket in her shirt, wrapping it carefully in a handkerchief from her backpack. Once the bags were full, they deposited them in a pile outside the door. Zoya surveyed the remaining gold, about three quarters of the original hoard. 'What are we going to do with this?'

'Leave it,' said Vaspine. 'The crystal's what we came for.'

'What if someone finds it?'

'They haven't been able to break in for ten years,' said Vaspine. 'Why should they be able to now? When everything with Kane has died down, we'll come back, grab what's left and give it to people who need it.'

'Like my dad would have wanted,' said Zoya.

Vaspine patted her back. 'Like your dad would have wanted.'

Zoya didn't say anything, but she felt warm inside. Vaspine led them out of the vault and together they lifted the gold-filled backpacks down the stairs and onto the grass. Once all their feet were off the staircase, the door slid back into place and clanged shut. The sound caught them by surprise and they turned to see what it was. When they realized, they each let out a laugh. 'Neat,' said Zoya.

'It is neat,' said a voice behind them. 'In fact, I'd say you've been pretty neatly tricked.'

Zoya, Vaspine, and Beebee turned around. Standing a few feet away was Lendon Kane and two of his men. They each held a gun, all pointed at Zoya.

Vaspine stepped in front of her. No sooner had he moved than Kane shifted the barrel of his gun in the captain's direction.

'Pass those here,' he said, nodding at the bags. Vaspine surveyed them, then bent to pick them up. He threw the first two to Kane, but as he picked up the third, Zoya noticed that he also scooped up a handful of gravel. He slipped this into his pocket, then tossed the final bag towards Kane's feet.

'Thank you,' said Kane. 'Such cooperation earlier might have rendered this unpleasantness unnecessary.'

'There won't be any unpleasantness,' said Vaspine, his eyes dripping fire. To his left, Beebee inched forwards, but Vaspine motioned for him to stop.

'You're wrong,' said Kane. 'So far I've been patient, but now my patience has run out.'

'So has mine,' snarled Beebee.

Kane shifted his gaze wearily to the big man. 'Tell your pit bull to quieten down,' he said, aiming his words at Vaspine, 'or I'll put a bullet through his cranium.'

Vaspine gestured for Beebee to be quiet.

'Did you really think you'd be able to run?' continued Kane. 'Did you really think your little trip through the Dalmacia Pass would be the end of it? All you've done, with all your scheming, is bring the locket here to me, right where I want it. And now, after ten years, the crystal is mine.' He smirked. 'I ought to thank you.'

Vaspine continued to stare, although Zoya could tell he was fingering the dust in his pocket. 'We didn't walk all this way to listen to you. Get out of our way.'

Kane fired a bullet into the air. 'Enough!' he roared. He fired a second bullet, then brought his gun down so it was pointed at Vaspine. 'You will give me the locket, and then you and your friends will die.'

Vaspine clenched his fists, then spoke to Beebee out of the corner of his mouth. 'Kane's mine. The others are yours, left and right. Take them out.'

'Don't you understand, Carlos?' growled Kane. 'There's no way out of this. You're beaten. All your plans, they're worthless.'

Vaspine glanced at Zoya. 'You'll know when to run. Keep going until you reach the ship. Don't look back. Tell Rosie to get away. OK?'

Zoya nodded.

Kane stepped forward and pointed his gun between Vaspine's eyes. 'You are going to die,' he shouted.

Vaspine smiled, then took a deep breath and answered calmly. 'Not today.'

As he said the words, the captain pulled the handful of gravel from his pocket and flung it in the eyes of Kane and his men. The pirates dropped their guns as Vaspine and Beebee charged, Beebee clattering into the pirate to Kane's left and Vaspine slamming into Kane's midriff.

Zoya watched all five tumble to the ground. Without thinking, she sprinted to a nearby copse, shot through the trees and continued up the hill towards the valley entrance. When she reached it, she ignored Vaspine's instruction and glanced back. She spotted the captain and Beebee wrestling in the grass and fought an urge to return.

When Zoya emerged onto the ridge, much of the fog had gone, as had the wind. From the platform, she could see all the way down the mountain to the forest. With her goal in sight, she redoubled her efforts, barrelling along the spur and dashing down the rocks. Every time she put her foot down she felt a sharp pain lance her knees, but she kept moving. She ran for an hour, until every muscle in her body burned and she felt like she couldn't take another step, then she slumped onto a boulder. She stayed there until she'd regained her breath, clutching the Algrond Crystal to her chest and counting backwards from ten, trying to calm her racing heart.

As Zoya navigated back to the woods, the sun was setting behind the hills. She glanced up the path to see if she could make out any figures following. All she could see were a few shapeless forms silhouetted against the sky, but it was too dark to be sure whether they were people and she didn't want to hang around to find out.

When Zoya tried to run again she found she could barely move, so she half-jogged, half-walked the last few miles to the ship. The first person to spot her was the Doc. Seeing him, Zoya dropped to her knees on the grass. The next few minutes were hazy. She could remember being carried up the gangplank, laid down on her bed and covered with a blanket. She could remember seeing Bucker's smiling face and hearing the Doc go to fetch Rosie.

Then everything went black.

Sometime later, she came to in a dim room. Around her were the outlines of shadowy figures. Gradually, her sight returned and she was able to recognize Bucker, Rosie, Cid, and the Doc. Zoya's bag lay beside Rosie, its contents spilled on the table. In her hand, Rosie cradled the Algrond Crystal. She handed this to the Doc, who rushed off towards his lab. Then Rosie turned to Zoya. The girl started to wrench herself up, but Rosie laid her back down. 'Rest,' she said. 'What's happened?'

Zoya whispered two words. 'Ambush. Kane.'

57

Cid leapt out of his seat. 'I knew it. I knew we shouldn't have let them go alone!'

Rosie gestured for him to calm down.

'No. This was a mistake. They never should have gone for that crystal. Beebee was right.'

'Maybe,' said Rosie, guiding Cid back to his seat. 'But we need to deal with the current situation, which means listening to Zoya.'

Cid sat down. 'Sorry, kid.'

Zoya blinked, her head still groggy. When she was ready, she cleared her throat. 'They ambushed us near the vault. We'd just loaded the bags and were about to come back . . .' She coughed. '. . . when they appeared behind us.'

'How many?' asked Rosie.

Zoya pictured them. 'Kane and two others.'

'Armed?' asked Cid.

Zoya nodded. 'I think. The last thing I remember is the captain telling me to run.'

'Do you know what happened to Beebee and the captain?'

Zoya thought back to the dark shapes on the horizon. 'There was someone on the mountain when I got to the bottom. I think.'

'That's good enough for me,' said Rosie, turning to Cid. 'We need to get them.'

'No,' cried Zoya. She sat upright.

Rosie stroked her hair. 'It's OK, you've told us enough.'

'No,' said Zoya, again.

'What is it?'

'The captain said no. Get us out of here,' Zoya croaked. 'He said to get away.' Zoya's words descended into coughs. Bucker darted out of his seat and handed her a glass of water.

Cid looked at Rosie. 'That damn fool! He wants us to leave.'

'And we won't,' said Rosie, her voice quivering. 'I should have gone in the first place. I'm sure as hell not leaving them now.'

Cid nodded. 'I'll gather the men.'

Rosie remained with Zoya as Cid left to organize a search party. She went through the details of the route to the vault, then left, instructing Bucker to keep watch. Zoya waited for a few minutes after she was gone, then swung her legs off the bed and staggered to her feet. She swayed momentarily, then steadied herself on the bedpost. Bucker tried to lay her back down, but Zoya brushed him off. 'We're here because of me,' she said, 'I'm going to do what I can.'

They found Rosie at the top of the gangplank surveying Cid's men, who were lined up on the grass below. The group included her best swordfighters, as well as Beebee's finest boxers. Each had a backpack and a weapon. She was just about to descend and address them when there was a shout from across the deck. 'Man down below.'

Rosie swept to the other side of the ship and leapt onto the gunwale. On the surface was a dishevelled and battered figure. Struggling to stand, he remained upright by leaning on the hilt of his sword and gripping at loose panels on the hull. Rosie smiled when she saw the man, for she knew him immediately—even with the cuts and the bruises and the blood-smeared face. 'Captain!' she shouted.

Zoya felt like crying in relief. She watched Vaspine make his way to the gangplank, ignoring the crew on the grass as he passed them, and also Rosie as she raced to meet him halfway up the platform. Rosie turned, a puzzled look on her face. The captain's movements were slow, and she soon caught him. 'Carlos, I'm so glad you're safe!'

'Is Zoya here?' he asked.

Rosie pointed her out, up on the deck. The captain paused to check with his own eyes, then continued.

'Did she have the crystal?'

Rosie nodded. 'What happened?'

Vaspine didn't respond.

'What happened? Where's Beebee?'

The captain continued. He'd reached the deck now and he let his sword drop to the wood, its blade smeared with blood. His hand was gashed and swollen where he'd leaned on the sword's hilt, and he had cuts all over his arms and neck. He limped to the bridge. 'Cid?'

The pilot squinted at the battered figure. 'Cap', is that you?'

'Cid, get us out of here.'

One glance at the captain's eyes convinced Cid he was serious, and he wheeled away, barking instructions at his deputies. Satisfied, Vaspine descended back to the deck and started to trudge towards his quarters. Rosie stepped in line with him near the wall of crates. 'Carlos, you need to tell me what's happened. Are we safe? Where's Beebee?'

Vaspine stopped. For the first time, Zoya was able to see his eyes—bloodshot against a patchwork of cuts and bruises. The captain stared at Rosie with a look so unbearable Zoya knew what he was going to say before he said it. Her breath fled. 'Beebee's dead, Rosie. He's dead.'

58

Vaspine walked away. Zoya felt like shouting after him, screaming that it was a lie, that Beebee was OK, but she knew he was telling the truth.

An entire minute passed before her legs felt steady enough to follow. She stumbled down the deck until she was standing in the doorway of Vaspine's quarters. The captain and Rosie were inside, Vaspine standing in front of the mirror, wiping blood from his face with a towel.

'What happened?' asked Rosie.

'Kane,' said Vaspine. His face tightened. He slumped into his chair near the skymap. 'This was what he wanted all along. He wanted us to take the locket to the vault, and I walked right into it.' He slammed his fist onto the map, scattering markers over the floor. 'He beat me.'

'He beat all of us,' said Rosie.

'But he was playing with *me*.'

Zoya entered the cabin, picked up one of the captain's discarded towels, rinsed it in the corner sink and brought it to him. She held it out until he took it, her eyes red and puffy. Vaspine forced a smile, and started to dab at his cuts. 'Tell me how,' said Zoya. 'I have to know.'

Vaspine sighed. When he spoke, his voice was calm. 'After you left, we fought. Beebee managed to take one out straight away. He knocked him off the steps. That left Kane and another guy. Beebee went after him and I was already on Kane. I'd knocked his gun away when I first hit him. I saw him pick it up, so I charged his middle again and dragged him to the ground. I managed to yank the gun out of his hand and throw it, but as I did he pulled a dagger. I had to get away, so I jumped to my feet and stumbled back. I knew I had a dagger tucked into my right boot, but I didn't have time to get it. He came quick and lunged at me. I just about knocked him aside, but he caught me . . .' Vaspine lifted his right forearm and revealed a gash that ran from his elbow to his wrist. 'It's not as bad as it looks, but I couldn't use that arm. The dagger was in my right boot, which meant I had to get it with my left hand. I waited for him to come again, then shrugged him off. That was my chance. I tried to pull it out. It was stuck. I really had to pull. When it came free, I turned around and he was already charging, so I braced myself . . .' he paused. 'Neither of us saw him coming.'

'Beebee,' said Rosie.

The captain nodded. 'He ran in front of Kane. I didn't see the knife go in, but I saw the blood. He dropped to the ground in front of me. His face was white.'

'And Kane?'

'I went for him' said Vaspine. 'But he ran. Beebee was wounded near his chest. The dagger must have pierced his heart.'

Rosie placed her hand on Vaspine's. 'It wasn't your fault, Carlos.'

'It was!' snapped the captain. 'I was the one who said we should go to the vault. Beebee knew it was a bad idea and he was brave enough to tell me. Now he's dead.'

'Carlos . . .'

'No!' shouted Vaspine. 'We shouldn't have gone.'

The captain's outburst made Zoya jump. Rosie crossed to her and put an arm around her. As she did, Zoya regarded the captain's face. It looked strange, as if he was somewhere else. 'What are we going to do?' she asked, eventually.

Vaspine rubbed his forehead. 'We fly until we're away from this island.'

'We have barely any money left,' said Rosie. 'And we're starting to run low on food.'

'We'll have no *anything* if Kane finds us here.'

Rosie eyed the captain carefully. 'Are you going to be all right, Carlos?'

'I don't think I'll ever be all right again.'

59

Zoya stumbled away from the captain's quarters, her face pale. She hunched over, shivering under the afternoon sun. 'No,' she heard herself say as she walked along. 'No, no, no.' She ran to her cabin and collapsed on her bed, her head buried in her pillow, sobs wrenching her body. For half an hour, she rocked backwards and forwards, until her sobs turned to whimpers. She covered herself with a blanket and lay under it, her mind racing with thoughts of Beebee.

Feeling sick, she went outside. Without thinking, she headed straight for Bucker's lookout pod. She found him crumpled in a corner, his eyes puffy and bloodshot. When he saw her, he wiped his tears. 'Are you all right?'

'Are you?' asked Zoya.

Bucker shook his head.

'Me neither,' said Zoya.

'I can't believe it. I keep expecting him to shout up.'

Zoya twisted her foot into the pod floor and stared into the distance, avoiding Bucker's gaze. 'He didn't want to go, you know? To the island. It was my decision. I made us. It's my fault.'

Bucker shook his head. 'No, it's Kane's fault. He's the one who's chasing us. It was him that killed Beebee. Kane's to blame. But we've got to do something or we *will* be to blame. That's what Beebee would have wanted.' Suddenly, Bucker grabbed Zoya's arm. 'He always said to fight the nasty ones, even when you don't want to. Because if you don't fight them, no one will.' He wiped his face. 'We need to go after him, Zoya. Make him pay.'

'They'll rip us apart,' said Zoya.

'They could rip any ship apart.'

'He might leave us alone now.'

'He might go after someone else.'

Bucker was right. Beebee had been right. Kane wouldn't give up. He'd chase them until he caught them, and when he did he'd destroy everything. Then he'd find something else to destroy. He'd continue to stalk the skies until somebody destroyed the *Shadow*, or somebody destroyed him.

Zoya was just about to tell Bucker this when she was thrown into the side of the pod. The ship around her dipped, pressing to starboard. When the movement stopped, Zoya pulled herself to the edge and looked down. A crowd of people had gathered around the bridge. Standing beside the wheel were Cid and the captain.

'What is it?' asked Bucker.

'I think,' said Zoya, scrutinizing the shifting cloud formations above her head, 'we're going somewhere.'

60

Zoya had traversed the rigging so many times now that she actually beat Bucker down to the deck for the first time. As Bucker's feet thudded onto the wood, he shot her a glance. 'The last time, I promise.'

From the mainmast, they advanced to the bridge. On their way, Zoya heard rapid footsteps over her shoulder. Rosie overtook them a moment later, her fists bunched at her sides. 'She looks mad,' said Zoya.

Bucker looked apprehensive. 'We'd better get over there.'

The captain and Cid were still beside the wheel when they arrived. At the bottom of the stairs sat the Doc, his eyes directed at the strip of solar sail in his lap. Rosie had jumped onto the starboard gunwale to their left and was eyeing the landscape around the ship. She shouted at the captain over her shoulder. 'What's going on? Where are we going?'

Vaspine looked across at her, then stepped down the stairs from the bridge. 'We're getting away.'

'To where?'

'Anywhere.'

Rosie shook her head. 'We'll never make it. We haven't fixed the ship. Doc, have you?'

The Doc glanced up from his work. 'Does it look like it?'

Rosie held out a hand as if she'd proved her point.

The captain sighed. 'We have to get away.'

Rosie stared at him as the ship creaked around them. Eventually, she spoke. 'You're scared.'

Vaspine's eyes flared. 'What do you want from me? Stay here and get everyone killed? Because that's what will happen if we stay. Sooner or later, he's going to find us here.' He glared at Rosie until she looked away, then rounded on the rest of the crew. His voice was sharp, commanding. 'Listen. All of you. There isn't a soul on this ship that wants to take Kane out more than me. But I don't fancy suicide and I don't imagine you do either.'

Zoya stared at them with blank eyes. Inside, an anger started to build. Flashes of fire coloured her vision, so hot she had to shake her head to clear them. She was sad. She was tired. But more than anything she was angry. A pang shot through her, at the thought of everything Kane had taken—the years she could have spent with her parents, gone because of Kane's greed. She thought of all the good people who'd looked after her, murdered, and her anger grew. All of a sudden, she exploded.

'Stop!'

Zoya walked to the centre of the crowd and faced the captain. 'We need to stop. We run, he follows. We run again, Beebee dies. He killed Mr Whycherley, my parents. Who's next? You? Rosie? Cid? Bucker? No more!' Zoya slammed her fist into the side of the bridge. 'Beebee was right. My dad was right. We have to fight Kane. You say he's been after this crystal all these years, he won't give in. We need to put an end to him once and for all. If we don't stand up to him, who will? How many more people will he kill before somebody stops him? It has to be us!'

Zoya panted as all the tension inside her dissipated. For the first time in days, she felt calm. She caught Bucker's smile out of the corner of her eye as the captain approached. 'Zoya,' said Vaspine, peering down, 'you and I were lucky to come back from the vault alive. Next time we might not be so lucky.'

'I don't care,' said Zoya. 'One way or another, Kane's hurt all the people who matter to me. To all of us. He has to pay.'

Vaspine turned to the rest of the crew. 'Do you agree?'

The crowd around him whispered. Heads started to nod.

'Yeah!'

'Yeah, I've had enough of this guy.'

'Nobody kills a *Dragonfly* and gets away with it.'

Vaspine bowed his head to indicate he'd understood. He glanced between Rosie and Cid, both of whom nodded. 'Very well,' he said. 'When the sun comes up, we aim for the *Shadow* and don't stop until its reign of terror ends. No matter the cost.'

61

With what little food remained, the ship partied late into the night. Vaspine declared it a duty for every crew member except the Doc to celebrate Beebee's life.

'So I get to spend an evening working on that ball of light while you guys have fun?' The Doc stomped off down deck, muttering under his breath. 'Very fair.'

Zoya joined the party. Beebee had meant a lot to her in the short time she'd known him. She wanted to give him the send-off he deserved.

Towards the end of the evening, she found herself alone with Cid at the stern of the ship. The pilot had deposited a jar of ale on the side and was rubbing his hand along the wood, smoking his pipe. He glanced back as Zoya approached. 'I'm thinking about getting a plaque made for Beebee. Stick it here.'

Zoya's eyes sparkled. 'That's a nice idea.'

'We ought to be getting one for you, what with you being

sky thief royalty and all.'

Zoya blushed and dropped her eyes. 'I'm just a girl.'

'Nonsense!' said Cid, blowing a ring of smoke. 'I knew there was something special about you the minute I saw you.'

Zoya smiled. Cid finished his pipe, tapped out the remaining ash and fitted it in his pocket. Retrieving his ale from the gunwale, he pecked Zoya once on the forehead. 'Don't worry, though, you'll always be a newbie to me.' With that, he winked and started to weave off down the ship.

* * *

The deck was almost empty when Zoya crawled out of her cabin in the morning. There were only three people outside—Cid, already at his post on the bridge and looking like he'd never touched a drop, and Rosie and Charlie sharing breakfast. Zoya walked over.

'Morning.'

'Where are we?' asked Zoya.

'Somewhere west of the Dalmacians,' said Rosie. 'We're on our way back to the Island in the Sky.'

'But I thought we were going after Kane.'

'We are. But first we need to work out where he's gone. Charlie's going down to ask.'

'I used to work in Moonfall,' explained Charlie when he saw the puzzled look on Zoya's face. 'Still got a few friends there.'

Zoya nodded.

'Charlie's going to jump off,' said Rosie, 'grab some supplies with what we've got left from the cruiser raid and call in a few favours to get the information. In the meantime, the Doc's going to fire up the new mini-sun.'

'And then?'

'The captain's working on that,' said Rosie. 'Now go and get some breakfast. You're going to need all your strength today.'

'But . . .'

'Go!'

Zoya gave in and headed for the mess hall. There was little left, but she was able to scrape together a couple of pieces of toast. By the time she'd finished, the *Dragonfly* was carving its way through the same air it had a couple of days before, approaching the Island in the Sky from the south. She thought back to that afternoon, sitting on Beebee's shoulders.

They came to a stop over a farmer's field a mile out of town. Charlie was already hooked up to a rope near the gunwale. Rosie boosted him over and winched him to the ground, before Cid lifted them back into the air.

'Right,' said Rosie, 'let's get this ship ready for battle.'

62

The chef returned later that evening. They met him where they'd left him and winched him up. Strapped across his back were four bags of supplies, which he immediately unloaded onto the deck. 'At last,' he said, rubbing his shoulders.

The captain was out on deck to meet him, along with Cid, Rosie, Zoya, Bucker, and most of the rest of the crew. However, it was Vaspine and Rosie that Charlie most wanted to speak to, and he pulled them aside as soon as he unhooked himself from the winch. Zoya followed, pretending to watch the sky.

'Where?' asked Vaspine, without preamble.

'The Dalmacia Pass,' said Charlie.

'Why there?'

'He figures we'll still go there to get away.'

'Your source,' said Vaspine, 'are they trustworthy?'

'As trustworthy as anyone down there.'

Vaspine looked at Rosie. 'What do you think?'

Rosie shrugged. 'It's the best we've got.'

'So be it,' said Vaspine. He dismissed Charlie with a nod, then called over Cid. 'How long to the Dalmacia Pass?'

'From here?' Cid tilted his head, calculating the Island in the Sky's movements relative to the pass. His face brightened. 'Four hours.'

'Make it happen.'

Cid nodded and walked off to the bridge, barking navigational orders at his deputies. With the pilot gone, Vaspine let out a sigh. 'We'll be at the pass, not with our tails between our legs as Kane's imagining it,' he said to Rosie, 'but with our swords drawn.' With that, he straightened his waistcoat and walked off. He'd moved only a short distance when he stopped and called over his shoulder. 'Rosie?'

'Captain.'

Vaspine glanced at Charlie's bags of supplies. 'Tell him double rations for everyone.'

The lunch was a quiet affair. Nobody made speeches. There were no battle cries. Indeed, nobody mentioned the upcoming battle at all. The atmosphere made Zoya feel prickly, so she excused herself and headed outside. A few hours had passed since Charlie's return, which meant they had to be approaching the Dalmacia Pass. Without intending to, she wandered to the spot at the stern where she'd taught Beebee to charm the birds. A couple of starlings were there when she arrived, fluttering about. Zoya watched them.

'I miss him already,' said a voice from behind.

248

Zoya turned to find Bucker standing by the bridge, a biscuit in each hand. He tossed one over. 'Couldn't let you miss your pud.'

Zoya smiled. 'Thanks.'

Off the port side, a flock of birds flew in the line with the ship, the light of its oil lanterns reflecting off their feathers.

'You OK?' asked Bucker.

'I'm OK,' said Zoya. 'Surprisingly. When Mr Whycherley died, I was angry. When Beebee died, I was angry. I don't feel like that now.'

'That's good,' said Bucker. He pulled himself onto the gunwale.

'Are you scared?' asked Zoya, abruptly.

Bucker scoffed. 'Me? Scared?'

Zoya arched an eyebrow.

He smiled. 'Of course. Everyone I love is about to pick a fight with the most frightening man in the world. I don't want anyone else to die.'

Bucker kicked his legs against the hull as Zoya pulled herself up. 'You know,' she said, 'Mr Whycherley always used to tell me I had a say in how I lived my life. He said I could do something with it. Here, on this ship, I'm doing something worthwhile for the first time. Most worthy things aren't easy, and getting rid of Kane's one of them. But I've come to realize that when there's bad in the world, someone's got to stand up to it, even if they're scared. That's what my dad did, and it's what I'm going to do.'

Bucker slapped her on the back. 'I'm proud of you Zo.'

Zoya grinned. The light had dimmed now, and she glanced down at Bucker's wristwatch. 'What time is it?'

'Huh?'

'It's getting dark early, isn't it?'

Bucker frowned. 'Weird.' He looked around. 'I wonder . . .' Bucker froze, his head angled to the sky. His face turned a horrible, sickly white.

'What?' asked Zoya, turning around. High above the *Dragonfly*, nestled amongst the nimbus clouds, hung an enormous, motionless, monolithic shape. Its bulk blocked the sunlight from reaching the ship, casting a gloom over everything on board. Zoya and Bucker stared open-mouthed, before slowly, almost imperceptibly, the shape started to descend.

'The *Shadow*!' said Bucker.

63

Of the adults, Cid was the first to react. He leaned back off the bridge and shouted to them. 'You two, get down now.'

Zoya helped Bucker down as Vaspine and Rosie emerged from the captain's quarters and started to stride across the deck. Vaspine collared a passing thief as he walked. 'Go and get the Doc. Bring him to me.'

'Is it . . . him?' asked the thief.

'The Doc, now!'

Vaspine stared at the giant ship, his face strained. He lingered a moment longer, then smirked. 'If you live by the sword, you die by the sword.'

Something in Vaspine's voice—some bloody-minded determination—cheered Zoya. She watched him spin from the *Shadow* and into action. 'Put on some armour!' he yelled at a nearby thief. 'Get yourself a weapon!'

Rosie issued orders too. 'Take these,' she said, handing off a bundle of swords to a passing thief. 'Make sure everyone gets one.'

'There aren't enough,' said the thief, his voice shaky.

'Tell those who don't get one to find something to defend themselves.'

The thief nodded and made his way down the deck, handing out a sword to anyone with empty hands. Zoya grabbed Bucker and dragged him towards Rosie. When Rosie saw her son, she threw her arms around him. 'What are you two doing here? You need to get below deck!'

'I'm staying,' said Zoya. 'It's my father's crystal Kane's after. I can't leave everyone else to fight.'

Rosie glared. 'Zoya . . .'

'I mean it!'

Rosie looked across at Bucker. 'I guess you're going to tell me the same.'

'Somebody's got to look after her,' he said.

Rosie sighed. 'OK, you've got about . . .' she glanced up at the *Shadow*, which had already covered half the distance to the *Dragonfly*, '. . . five minutes before this ship'll be swarming with Kane's men.'

Zoya raced to her cabin and picked up Storm. She strapped the blade to her body, checked the locket was secure and made her way back outside. The deck was full now, with thieves running to their places, preparing for battle. In the middle Vaspine was questioning the Doc.

'All I want to know,' said Vaspine, 'is whether you've restarted the mini-sun?'

The Doc squirmed. 'It's flaming. But there's still only one sail.'

'Yes or no?'

The Doc sighed. 'We won't be as fast as we were, but it'll be close.'

'That'll do,' said Vaspine. He shoved past the Doc towards Cid. The pilot was leaning against the ship's wheel, calm as ever. Around his neck hung his lucky goggles, and he was tossing a coin in his hand. When he saw the captain, he flipped the coin high in the air and caught it in a closed palm.

'Heads we get out of this one,' he said.

'Tails they don't,' said the captain, with a smile. 'Cid, make no mistake old friend, this one's on you. If you don't fly like you've never flown before, we don't stand a chance.'

Cid smiled and slotted the coin into his pocket. 'Now that's a challenge.' He stepped across to the wheel.

'Cid,' the captain stopped him. 'Whatever it takes.'

Cid nodded. Vaspine spun back to Rosie, who was huddled with her swordfighters. When she heard Vaspine call, she dismissed them. 'Captain?'

'The plan is to get them on here,' he said. 'When they come, go for the biggest and take them out.' Vaspine narrowed his eyes.

'And after him?'

'The next biggest,' said Vaspine. 'Work your way down until the only people left are the ones meant to be here. Clear?'

'Clear.'

Vaspine whirled around again, this time taking in the entire airship and going through a checklist in his head. After a few more barked orders, he seemed happy that everything was in place. It was then he nodded to himself and started in the direction of his cabin. Rosie noticed this. 'What are you doing?'

Vaspine looked at her for a moment without speaking. 'The stupidest thing I've ever done.'

Then he was gone.

64

Zoya and Bucker were left alone. Zoya looked for something to do, but everyone was already busy with jobs of their own. She searched around the deck for Rosie, and found her jamming spikes into the outside of the hull. 'Rosie,' she shouted, 'can we help?'

Rosie slammed in a final spike and started to march away. 'Come with me.'

Zoya and Bucker followed her back to the stern, where Cid and a few of his deputies were huddled around a map. 'He's going to try to finish this before we're ready, so we have to stop him. We're going to drop low,' he said. 'It'll be harder for him to keep up. I want you people to be my eyes. What you see, I need to see. You've got to tell me everything—hills, clock towers, trees, waterfalls, boulders, mountains. Heck, even cows if they're in my way.'

Cid shooed them away with a swipe of his arm and started to guide them into viewing positions within earshot of the bridge. He sent Zoya to a spot on the starboard side, and

Bucker to the same place on the port side. They jumped into position. Once Cid was happy, he stepped behind the wheel, straightened his goggles, lit his pipe and took a grip. 'Good luck, everyone.'

He gunned the engines. For the first time in days, Zoya felt the power of the *Dragonfly* burn up her spine, throwing her and many of the lookouts to the deck. The Doc smiled as he clung to a mast, happy to have helped even if he'd never admit it. Of them all, only Cid remained upright, his hands wrapped around the wheel and his back straight as a tree trunk. Zoya dragged herself back to a standing position, only to feel another lurch as the ship started to descend rapidly. She managed to pull herself to the gunwale and glance over the side. The ship was skimming along at an altitude of a hundred feet.

Cid rocked the ship left and right, dropped it down and dragged it up, all based on the information of his deputies. Rosie joined the spotters, repeating anything she thought Cid might have missed in the engine's roar. When she got a moment, Zoya glanced back at the *Shadow*, which was only a mile behind now, lower in the sky than it had been before. Whilst he waited for the captain's return, Cid tried a series of evasive manoeuvres. But it was no good. Every time he thought he'd found a gap too small for the *Shadow* to follow, Kane would smash through anyway. 'The guy's a maniac,' shouted Cid, after the *Shadow* had destroyed another bridge.

'That's what we're counting on!'

Zoya turned around to see the captain. Wrapped around one of his arms was a length of bungee rope and in the other he held a clamp. He dumped the gear on the deck and leapt onto the bridge. 'How are we doing?' he asked.

'How does it look?' said Cid.

Vaspine squinted at the horizon. 'You're still heading into the Dalmacia Pass, yes?'

'I'm trying,' said Cid, 'if everyone would stop interrupting me!'

The captain laughed.

'Take the ship east, there's a canyon beyond that ridge. A shortcut. Fly us in there, then let them get close.'

'I know the shortcut,' snapped the pilot. 'Why the hell do you want me to go in there? We'll be sitting ducks!'

'Just trust me,' said Vaspine. 'If we don't do this, we're dead anyway.'

65

Cid growled, but swung the wheel to starboard as ordered. The airship followed, cutting a deep valley into the forest below. A minute or so later, they plunged through the shortcut's opening as Zoya leaned over the side to get a look. They were rushing down a narrow passage flanked by mammoth walls of granite that rose to the sky. Jutting out of these were river-houses carved into bulging ridges, their owners peering out from inside. Below, a glassy river meandered through the canyon, twisting with the rock. A few boats that had been gliding downstream were tossed around in the airship's wake.

'He's not going to be able to avoid those people,' said Zoya.

'It's not Cid you need to worry about,' said Rosie. 'He could fly a bathtub in a tornado. It's Kane. He won't care.'

Zoya glanced back in time to see the *Shadow* crash through the canyon's opening. The gorge was narrower at its mouth than mid-stream, and its granite walls scraped at Kane's airship as it squeezed through. Once inside, the *Shadow* took a moment to right itself, before accelerating after the *Dragonfly*. To her right, the captain cheered and pumped his fist in the air. 'They bought it!'

'Bought what?' asked Zoya, but Vaspine had already moved on.

'Rosie?'

'Captain.'

'We've got one chance at this. I want you to get the crew ready to fight. Kane's men will be here in a few minutes.'

Rosie nodded. Vaspine smiled, then turned away. Before he could move, he was flung to the deck by a jolt that shunted the entire airship. Almost everybody on board went down with him, including Zoya, who banged her head on the corner of a lantern. Darkness descended for a few moments, then she woke to find herself flat-out on the deck. She rubbed her head and tried to sit up, but a sharp pain flashed across her forehead and she collapsed again. The only person left standing was Cid.

'What was that?' asked Zoya, but she knew the answer. Above Cid's head and to the right loomed the black and red hull of the *Shadow*, a dent in the metal where it had rammed the *Dragonfly*. Protruding from the ship's front was its bowsprit, this carved into the shape of a large dagger. Perched on the blade's tip, the wind rushing through his hair and a maniacal grin on his face, was Lendon Kane.

'If I'd known I could topple you all with one shunt, I'd not have bothered preparing my men,' he said.

Vaspine climbed to his feet. Zoya did the same.

'Ah, you *are* there,' sneered Kane.

'It's over,' said Vaspine. 'We're going to finish this.'

'Finish this?' Kane laughed. 'In that wreck? I think not.'

'It's over, Lendon,' shouted Vaspine.

Kane stopped laughing, sprung to his feet and balanced on the end of the figurehead. He unsheathed his sword and aimed it at the *Dragonfly*. 'The old man couldn't stop me, what makes you think you could do any better?' Kane twisted the end of his moustache. 'You know, Carlos,' he said, pacing the length of the dagger, 'until your little mascot ran from me at the vault, I was going to let your crew live. I genuinely was.' He smirked. 'But no more. For the insult and inconvenience, every one of you will die.' Kane whirled a hand around his head and motioned towards the *Dragonfly*. 'Ram them to the ground.'

With that, he disappeared into the *Shadow*.

Vaspine turned to Cid. 'This is it, pal. Can you get above him?'

'Above?' Cid took a drag on his pipe. 'Hell cap', why don't I just run her into the canyon and be done with it?'

'Yes or no?'

'Probably,' said Cid. 'No,' he corrected himself, 'make that, if we're lucky. You know, what the heck! If I do I'm a hero and if I don't we all die anyway so no one finds out. Course I can!'

Vaspine smiled. 'You're a positive man.'

'I'm positive you're trying to kill me.' The pilot threw up his hands. 'Go on! I'll fly you above her, but this plan of yours better work.'

'It will.' Vaspine turned to Cid's deputies, who were still providing navigational information. 'I need a volunteer.'

Bucker thrust himself forward. 'We'll do it. Me and Zoya.'

Vaspine looked at Zoya, who nodded, then at Rosie. 'They're as safe with you as they are anywhere else on the ship,' she said.

Vaspine gathered up the lengths of rope and clamp he'd deposited on the deck. 'You two,' he said, pointing at the kids, 'come with me.'

66

They followed Vaspine to a quiet spot on the starboard side, where he dumped the equipment and leaned over the gunwale to get another look at the *Shadow*. The ship was still behind them, but gaining by the second as Cid slowed the *Dragonfly* ready for the manoeuvre.

'What's the plan?' asked Zoya.

'Kane won't risk sending his men on board while he can just ram us out of the sky. So we're going to take that away from him.'

'Why are we slowing down?'

'Sometimes, you have to give a little to gain some,' said Vaspine. He dropped down and ran to the other side of the airship, pulled himself onto the gunwale, looked again at the *Shadow*, then jogged back to Zoya and Bucker. 'Listen, we don't have time to discuss this,' he gathered up the clamp and ropes and started to attach them to a nearby metal plate. 'I need you to watch this.'

'Where are you going?' asked Bucker.

'To the *Shadow*.'

Zoya and Bucker gasped. 'On your own?' asked Zoya.

'It's a one-man job,' said the captain. He pointed to a spot on the *Shadow*'s hull. The ship was swinging into position, ready to ram the *Dragonfly*. 'Do you see that pump?'

Zoya nodded.

'It's called an Injektor. It's how they fly a ship that big. I'm going to take it out. When they can no longer move, Kane will send his men on board, and . . .'

'And then we fight,' finished Zoya.

The captain tugged at the clamp to check it was firmly attached. Once he was happy, he clipped the cord around his waist. 'How do I look?'

'Magnificent,' said Bucker.

'I'm going to jump down, smash their Injektor and then you two will reel me back in. Does that make sense?'

Zoya and Bucker nodded.

Vaspine pulled himself onto the gunwale ready to jump, then cupped his hands and shouted. 'Cid?'

'Captain?'

'Now!'

Zoya felt a sudden jerk as the *Dragonfly* rapidly decelerated. As the ship slowed, Cid pushed it upwards and to port, towards the *Shadow*. 'Right above them Cid,' yelled Vaspine.

'I'll get above you in a minute!'

The captain laughed as Cid wrestled with the wheel, trying to control the ship as it climbed. Momentarily, the *Dragonfly* drifted too close to the canyon wall and Cid had to yank it away, then he continued to drive it upwards until it was above the *Shadow*. He gripped the wheel as tight as he could to steady the ship, then yelled at the captain. 'You've got a minute. After that, they're going to know what you're up to.'

67

Vaspine plunged backwards off the ship. Zoya and Bucker rushed to see where he was. They spotted him a moment later, thudding into the *Shadow*'s hull. He bounced a couple of times, before they lost him against the dark of the airship. He reappeared close to the Injektor. He hooked himself to the gadget so he wouldn't be shaken off, then set about trying to prise it off, slotting his dagger between the metal and the hull and pulling with all his strength.

Zoya glanced up at the *Shadow*'s deck, where Kane appeared to have noticed something was wrong. He paced backwards and forwards along his ship, leaning over the side and trying to work out where Vaspine had attacked. When he eventually spotted the captain, he threw his hands into the air and gestured for two of his crew to deal with him.

The pair tossed a line over the edge of the *Shadow* and started to rappel down. Others picked up objects and threw them in the direction of Vaspine, who did his best to dodge them as he fought to dislodge the Injektor.

'We need to help him,' said Bucker.

Zoya looked around. Leaning against the gunwale was a bag of leftover wood scraps they'd used to repair the hull. 'Here.' She tossed a few to Bucker. 'Throw these.'

Zoya grabbed a handful of her own and started to lob them at the two pirates shimmying towards Vaspine. Most shots missed, but every now and then a chunk struck one on the shoulder or whistled past an ear, causing them to slow down or adjust their positions. 'Hurry up, captain,' she muttered.

Below, Vaspine was still grappling with the Injektor. Each second, the two pirates crawled closer. 'He's not going to make it!' shouted Zoya. No sooner had she yelled than Vaspine managed to prise off the Injektor's cover, sending it spiralling to the ground. With one hand he swiped at the pirates as they tried to knock him off, while with the other he slashed at the Injektor, drawing sparks that swelled into flames, before exploding into a giant fireball that engulfed most of the underside of the *Shadow*.

'No!' screamed Zoya, as Bucker's mouth dropped open. They watched the fireball mushroom, scudding along the keel and licking its sides. Great plumes of smoke billowed from where the Injektor had been. Zoya felt sick. 'No.'

'Reel it in!' shouted Bucker.

Zoya ran to the clamp and set the reel in motion. Yard after yard of rope wound around the spindle, but there was no sign of the captain. 'Come on,' she moaned.

Then, out of a gap in the smoke, burst the end of the captain's bungee cord. Attached, coughing and spluttering, was Vaspine.

The kids grabbed the captain as soon as he was close enough and hauled him over the edge of the ship. He collapsed on his back on the deck, sucking in gulps of air. Zoya and Bucker worked to unclip the smoking bungee cord from his waist. After a few more breaths, the captain stumbled to his feet and shook his head to clear the cobwebs.

'What now?' asked Zoya.

'Now?' said the captain, grinning. 'Now, we fight.'

68

The *Shadow* was close enough to the *Dragonfly* now to make out individual figures on board. Zoya snatched up a pair of binoculars and aimed them at the ship. Its deck was crawling with men, each busy kitting himself out ready to board.

Vaspine led Zoya and Bucker back to the bridge, where Rosie had lined up the rest of the crew, each armed and covered in what armour they could find. She handed Vaspine his gear, which he slipped over his shoulders before dropping in line with the others. Behind her, Zoya heard a loud clank. She turned around in time to see a metal hook the size of her forearm lock onto the other side of the ship. She ran over. The hook was attached to a wire that ran back to the *Shadow*. Already spidering along the wire were two of Kane's men. 'They're coming.'

Zoya returned to the others as Rosie started to walk up and down the line, gesturing for the thieves to ready their weapons. Zoya and Bucker remained at the front with

Vaspine. Another thirty seconds passed, then she heard a loud banging on the hull near the hooks, and a scratching as Kane's men dragged themselves up. Zoya glanced at the *Shadow*, where Kane stood with his arms folded, an impatient tilt to his head, his entire attention fixed on the *Dragonfly*. Zoya wrapped her hand around Storm.

When Rosie returned, she guided Zoya and Bucker to the back of the line. 'Stay here.'

Zoya drew her sword. It felt strange to think she might use it on another human at any moment. The appearance of a hand on the gunwale jolted her awake. She realized she'd been holding her breath and tried to let it out, but it caught in her throat. She waited. Another hand joined the first, then another and another. As Kane's men started to clamber over, Vaspine exchanged a glance with Rosie. They both nodded.

'So it goes,' he whispered, and he shifted his attention to the rest of the crew. He raised his sword. 'For Beebee!'

The sky thieves returned his cry. 'For Beebee!'

As one, the crew of the *Dragonfly* rushed forwards, leading with their swords, slashing at everything nearby. Kane's men were so astonished by the ferocity of the assault that they leapt back, suddenly hesitant. Vaspine and Rosie led the charge, as Zoya raced to catch up, all the anger detonating inside of her. The biggest of Kane's men—an ugly, muscular, bald pirate with a chain through his nose—

let out a war cry, a deep, rumbling roar that cut straight through Zoya. He started to push his comrades, one by one, towards the sky thieves.

Vaspine pressed ahead, hacking at a pirate who came within his reach, his dagger lacerating the man across the forearm. The pirate dropped his weapon and sunk to the deck, clutching his wrist, as Vaspine turned to fight another. This one he loomed over, his dagger raised, and swung early, slitting the man across the shoulder and propelling him into a metal rail. At this point, Rosie and Zoya joined the captain, and one by one they managed to dispatch the invaders, save for the pirate with the chain and another, younger pirate. Rosie moved towards them, but Vaspine held her back. He approached the pirate with the chain. 'We don't want to hurt any more people than necessary. Surrender.'

The pirate spat on the deck. 'If I surrender to you, Kane kills me anyway. I might as well die here.' He rushed the captain, who'd lowered his weapon. Vaspine tried to raise it in time to block the incoming blow, but Zoya realized he wouldn't make it and leapt across with Storm in the air, aimed at the pirate's chest. A wave of recognition passed across the man's face as he realized what was about to happen, and he tried to shift his bodyweight in mid-air. But it was too late. The man landed on the sword, a puzzled look on his face, before slumping to the deck.

Zoya felt dizzy. She tried to swallow, but her throat was

dry. Before she could work out what to think, Rosie clapped her on the back. 'Good work.'

Vaspine nodded, then regarded the final pirate. 'My offer still stands.'

'I s-s-surrender,' said the pirate, letting his dagger fall to the deck.

Vaspine dipped his head and Rosie stepped forwards and began to tie up the pirate. As she worked, the captain turned his attention to the rest of the airship, but his crew had fared equally well. 'Easy,' said Zoya, approaching from behind.

'That was wave one,' said Vaspine. He sucked blood from a cut on his knuckle. 'There'll be more.'

From across the gap that divided the two airships came the sound of slow clapping. In the centre of the *Shadow*'s deck, calm in his suit, stood Kane. He continued to clap until he had the attention of everyone on board the *Dragonfly*. 'Well done,' he said, aiming the words at Vaspine. 'But let's see how you fare a second time.' A look of irritation flashed across his face, then he turned to his men. 'Everyone who's left, board. First person to bring me the locket and the crystal gets half the gold!'

Immediately, Kane's men started to rush towards the wires. Kane turned back to the *Dragonfly* and stared directly at Zoya. 'See you shortly.'

69

Rosie sheathed her sword. 'How long have we got?'

'A couple of minutes,' said Vaspine. 'Let's make them count. Re-arm, and get ready.'

Rosie headed off straight away. Vaspine spun around. 'Where's Zoya?'

'Here,' she said.

'He wants you in particular. We can't keep you safe and fight at the same time. We need to get you hidden——'

'I want to board the *Shadow*,' said Zoya.

Vaspine stopped mid-sentence. 'Don't be ridiculous.'

'I mean it,' said Zoya. 'If I get over there and finish him, I'll put an end to it all and no one else has to die.'

The captain shook his head. 'It's too dangerous. We'll deal with the next wave, then we'll board the *Shadow* together.' He turned to walk away, then stopped. 'Zoya, go to my cabin.'

Zoya leapt forward to argue, but Bucker grabbed her. A

glint in his eye warned her to stay quiet. 'I'll walk you over there,' he said.

'Hurry. Go now,' said Vaspine.

Bucker grabbed Zoya's hand and dragged her in the direction of the crew's quarters. When they were far enough away to talk without being heard, Zoya jerked him to a halt. 'What's going on?'

Bucker peered over his shoulder. 'Sometimes, you've got to fly against the wind,' he said. 'Let's find a way onto the *Shadow*.'

'You can't come,' said Zoya. 'It's dangerous!'

'Like heck!' said Bucker. 'You think I'd let you go alone?'

'This is my job,' said Zoya. 'You need to stay here.'

'Either I come with you or I march right up to the captain and tell him your plan.'

Zoya glanced at Vaspine, who was busy issuing orders. She had no choice. 'OK, come on. I've had an idea.'

Zoya led Bucker from the main deck, past the captain's quarters and around to the front of the ship. When they arrived, she opened the hatch that led to the lower decks and jumped down. Bucker followed. Zoya led him through the darkness, until they came upon the section of the hull they'd repaired a few days before. Sharp beams of light streamed through the few holes they'd missed. Bucker curled his lip. 'This is your great plan?'

Zoya ignored him and drew her sword. With its hilt, she battered at one of the remaining holes until, at first splinters, then entire panels, came away. After a minute, she'd managed to enlarge the hole so it was big enough for them to fit through. 'Look.'

Bucker peered through the gap. Six feet away was the metal hull of the *Shadow*. Level with them was a row of glass portholes that stretched the length of the airship. Seeing these, Bucker banged an excited hand on the wood. 'Now I get you.' For a moment, he seemed to think, then he jerked his head. 'Wait here.' Bucker disappeared down the passage and returned dragging one of his mother's gym benches. As soon as Zoya saw it, she understood his plan and went to help. They lugged the bench until it was level with the gap, then dropped it. Bucker positioned himself at the end furthest from the hole. 'Give me a hand.'

Zoya moved into position and took some of the weight. With a heave, they lifted the bench off the ground, guided the free end through the hole and into the gap between the two airships. With both of them at the same end, the bench was extremely heavy. Zoya moved so she was closer to the centre, but it made little difference. They needed to move fast.

Bucker took a breath. 'Three, two, one . . .'

They thrust the bench towards the nearest porthole. The wooden edge smashed through the glass first time, travelled a foot into the ship and lodged on the bottom of the frame. 'Bingo,' said Bucker.

Zoya rattled the bridge to check it was secure, then started to edge along its length, avoiding glancing at the emptiness below. Carefully, they crawled across the gap, then through shards of glass that ringed what was left of the window frame and into the *Shadow*. They emerged into a big, bright room, with scattered ale bottles and food piled high. As soon as they dropped down, Zoya turned to Bucker. 'I can do this on my own. Please go back.'

'I've come this far,' said Bucker, waving her away. 'I'm not leaving now.'

Zoya sighed. They left the room and made their way through the ship — cautiously at first, tiptoeing and peeking around every corner so as not to alert any pirates. However, once they'd navigated a few corridors, they realized they were alone——Kane seemed to have sent his entire crew onto the *Dragonfly*——and moved freely. A corkscrew of staircases led to the upper holds. Zoya and Bucker followed them until they arrived at the ship's mess hall. Through a window, Zoya spotted the main deck. She raced over and ducked down.

'Great,' said Bucker. 'What now?'

Zoya glanced through the window. 'It's time to end this.'

Zoya searched for a way outside and found a door to her right. She crawled over, stood up, checked to make sure Bucker was still following and then stepped out. The sunlight dazzled her as she emerged, reflecting off the metal. The only thing she could see clearly was the deck of the *Dragonfly*, upon which stood Vaspine, Cid, and Rosie. Scattered about them were clumps of Kane's men, tied together with rope. There were bodies too—some Kane's thieves, some Vaspine's thieves. Zoya winced at the sight, and felt like charging at Kane there and then.

But she couldn't.

She had to do this right.

She sucked in a lungful of air and started to head towards the centre of the deck. After a moment, her eyes began to adjust and she was able to make out the silhouette of a familiar shape ahead. Tall, thin, with the outline of a top hat, Zoya recognized Kane without taking another step. She drew Storm and pointed it at the figure. 'Kane,' she said, stepping confidently into his path, 'I've got you.'

70

A scream rang out from the *Dragonfly*. Rosie dropped to her knees. Vaspine darted over to see what had happened, only to notice Zoya and Bucker on the *Shadow*. He mouthed a silent 'no'.

Kane used the distraction to make a move. It was only the tiniest of flicks, but it was enough to allow him to pull a small lever on a panel next to his hands. Zoya saw the movement out of the corner of her eye, but it was too late to do anything. A pale blue light enveloped the ship, wrapping around it like a blanket and disappearing above their heads. It left behind a pulsating glow that stretched from the hull to a point level with the mainmast, some thirty feet above deck.

'On the contrary,' said Kane, turning to face Zoya. 'I've got you.'

Zoya looked again at the haze surrounding the airship, then back at Kane.

'That's a shield,' explained Kane. 'It's seldom used as my

ship is seldom attacked. Those who try have a nasty habit of dying.'

On the *Dragonfly*, Vaspine had recovered from the initial shock of seeing Zoya and Bucker. 'Hold him off, Zoya,' he yelled. 'I'm coming.'

'I think not, actually,' said Kane. 'It would take all the energy in Dalmacia to break through this shield. No, the girl's on her own.' He glanced at Rosie, who had climbed back to her feet, her fists bunched before her chest. 'Your boy, too.'

'Don't listen,' shouted Vaspine. 'Just hold him off!'

Vaspine scoured the deck for something heavy to throw. He spotted a stack of ale barrels nearby and headed over, beckoning two crew members to follow. Together, they grabbed a barrel and tossed it as hard as they could at the haze surrounding the *Shadow*. The barrel crashed into the force-field, making a static, crackling sound, sending sparks around the barrels like vines climbing a tree. The field bent inwards where the barrel hit, absorbed its kinetic energy, held the barrel for a moment, then spat it back at the *Dragonfly* as if it was a pebble. Vaspine watched it fall just short of the hull and plummet towards the ground.

'As I said,' sighed Kane, 'it would take all the energy in Dalmacia.'

Vaspine ignored him and started to search for something heavier. On the *Shadow*, Kane turned his attention to

Zoya and Bucker. He removed his top hat and suit jacket and deposited them on a nearby cannon. This done, he unbuttoned his shirt sleeves and rolled them above his elbows. Something about the calm, methodical way he did this sent a shiver down Zoya's spine.

'One way or another,' said Kane, moving towards Zoya and drawing his sword, 'you and your shipmates have given me quite the run-around over this locket.' He continued to advance, forcing Zoya and Bucker to back up towards the dining hall. 'The crystal too. Not many people have stopped me getting what I want. But I'm afraid your luck's come to an end.' He glanced at Bucker. 'Both of yours. You're going to hand me the locket,' he jabbed his blade at Zoya's neck, 'and then you and your friends are going to die.'

A clap to her left caused Zoya to jump as another object from the *Dragonfly* slammed into the force-field. Vaspine frowned as the object fell away. He held out his hands, appealing to the Doc for a plan. The Doc shook his head.

Zoya did her best to ignore them and kept her eyes fixed on Kane. 'Over the last few weeks,' she said, shakily, 'you and your men have killed two of the most important people in my life.' Zoya started to advance, causing Kane to hesitate. 'And before that, you killed my parents. I promise you, I am going to put an end to the *Shadow* once and for all.'

Kane hissed and launched himself blade-first at Zoya, teeth bared and a snarl on his lips. Zoya stepped aside, causing Kane to slide past her right shoulder and bounce off the wall. He tumbled to the ground like a sack of flour, sword in his hand, still aimed at Zoya. Zoya used the chance to dart away, blocking Kane's sword as she ran. But Kane was quick, and as Zoya backed away he got to his feet and started to advance. He swung his sword wildly, up and down. Zoya dodged the swipes as best she could, ducking first one way, then another, rolling under the blade. From across on the *Dragonfly*, she heard the sound of Vaspine throwing whatever he could at the force-field, but it seemed to hold. Over Kane's shoulder, Bucker stood near the mess hall, rooted to the ground.

Kane drove forwards, jabbing and swiping faster than Rosie ever had in training. Zoya parried the blows with Storm and tried to land a few of her own, but Kane was too powerful and so much bigger that Zoya couldn't get anything through. It was taking all of her strength just to block. She continued to back up, positioning a table between them and forcing Kane to stumble as he landed a jab. Zoya glanced over her shoulder. Behind her was a wall of netting. Instantly, she made a decision to sprint for it while Kane was picking himself up. She leapt into the air and gripped the rigging above her head. Every time she grabbed a new rung it scraped at her palms, but she ignored the burning and dragged herself up until she was at the top. As she hoisted herself over the cross-beam, Kane arrived below. Zoya glanced at him, down at the deck and jumped.

She dropped through the air like a cannonball and landed on the deck with a *thud*. Pain shot through her left ankle, but she ignored it and started to back away again. Kane looked up at the net, laughed quietly and slashed at it with his sword. Zoya's heart sank. Within seconds, Kane had created a hole big enough to fit through. 'You can't escape Zoya. You might as well give up.'

Kane squeezed sideways through the netting, then raised his sword. Zoya groaned and lifted Storm, which felt like a barbell, tugging at her arms. She limped backwards, purposefully toppling objects — chairs, tables, chests, sacks, lanterns—anything to slow Kane down. Kane sneered at Zoya's efforts and kicked the items aside.

Behind Zoya were the steps that led up to the bridge. She came upon them quicker than expected and felt her heel clip on the bottom step before she could adjust her footing. She stumbled backwards and landed on her backside. A smirk slipped across Kane's face when he realized he had Zoya trapped, and he raised his sword in victory. Zoya groped behind her head for something to throw. Halfway up the stairs was a discarded ale mug. She leaned back, grabbed the mug, swung it around and launched it at Kane's shins. The cup crashed into Kane's leg with a crack, causing him to double over in pain.

Zoya took her chance. She swung Storm at Kane's blade, catching it just above the hilt. The connection sent a jolt through her shoulder and down her arm, but it wrenched Kane's sword from his grip and sent it skidding down the steps back towards the rigging. A look of incomprehension flooded Kane's face, then anger when he realized what had happened. He reached inside his waistcoat and pulled out a dagger the length of Zoya's forearm. With a sneer, he launched himself towards Zoya, who leapt out of the way and banged into the ship's wheel. Winded, she clung to the wheel and dragged herself around until it stood between her and Kane.

Kane tried to circle the wheel to get at Zoya, but she managed to stay just out of range. Kane stepped away from the wheel, then launched himself at it again, this time jabbing his dagger through the spokes. It took Zoya a moment to realize what was happening, and one of the first stabs sliced open her waistcoat and nicked her ribs. She winced, and reached down to touch the wound. A trickle of blood seeped down her side, but the cut wasn't deep and she shook her head to clear away the pain. Kane pounced again, but Zoya was ready this time and she slipped and ducked as Rosie had taught her. Eventually, Kane became so frustrated that he vaulted onto the wheel to stab her over the top. Instinctively, Zoya stepped aside, but she stepped too far and tumbled over the edge of the platform, falling ten feet through the air and landing heavily on her back.

The wind left Zoya's chest for the second time in a minute,

and she lay on the deck, choking and gasping. During the fall, she'd let go of Storm and it lay away from her now, out of reach. Above, silhouetted against the sun, was Kane. He leaned over the edge, spotted Zoya and leapt down with his dagger. As he landed, he slid across the deck so he was positioned between Zoya and her sword. Satisfied, he started to straighten his clothes and smooth his hair. 'Did anyone tell you about your parents before they died? About how they begged for mercy before I killed them?' Kane waited for a response, but none came. 'You'll do the same,' he said. He started to advance. 'I'm going to enjoy this.'

Suddenly, Zoya noticed a movement over Kane's shoulder. She craned her neck to see what it was, causing Kane to do the same. Behind him, charging as fast as he could, was Bucker, his dagger raised. He clattered into Kane, and together they tumbled to the deck, Bucker on top, pounding with his fists and slashing with his knife. He struck a blow on the top of Kane's right arm, cutting through his shirt and deep into his flesh.

Kane roared. He dragged himself to his feet with Bucker still clinging on and tossed him against the side of the ship. Bucker hit the wall head-first and slumped to the deck, motionless. 'No!' screamed Zoya.

She leapt across the deck towards Storm, but Kane was there first and forced her up onto the gunwale. Kane followed, his sword aimed at Zoya's throat.

Zoya felt unsteady. She glanced over her shoulder at the dizzying drop and the hairs on her neck stood tall. She shut her eyes and tried to breathe. As she did, Kane took a swipe with his sword, forcing Zoya to leap back. Behind her was a platform that extended from the gunwale, hanging over the sky, barely wide enough to stand on.

Kane leapt onto the platform with Zoya, driving her into the force-field surrounding the ship. Zoya half expected the field to electrocute her as it had the barrel, but instead she passed through it as if it was made of air. She was a foot away from the end of the platform now, with only the clouds and Kane for company.

'Nowhere to go but down,' said Kane.

Zoya looked down once more, then back at Kane. From over on the *Dragonfly*, she heard Rosie shout the word, 'now!' It took Zoya a moment to realize what the older woman was talking about, then it hit her. She thought back to their training sessions in the gym—the long, sweaty hours—and remembered what Rosie had said about using all levels in a battlefield—left, right, up and *down*.

Zoya smiled. 'That's what I'm counting on.'

She took a step to her left and dropped off the platform out of sight. As she fell, she grabbed the edge of the plank with her left hand and used her momentum to swing under and around it just like Rosie had demonstrated. As she drove herself up the other side, she used her right hand to lift herself over the lip of the platform and back into a crouching position. As she landed, she barrelled into Kane's legs, causing them to buckle and sending him tumbling over the edge of the platform. Without thinking, Zoya thrust out an arm for Kane to grab. Kane shot out his own and gripped Zoya's. His weight pulled her onto the platform. Holding tightly with her free arm, Zoya was able to stop them both from plummeting.

'Hold tight little girl,' hissed Kane. 'If I fall, so do you.'

Kane's fingers dug into Zoya's wrist. Her chest was pulled so tight to the platform that she struggled to fill her lungs. She shifted her position to take some of the weight. As she did, her locket slipped out from beneath her shirt and dangled just in front of Kane's face.

Kane's eyes flashed. Then he released Zoya's arm and swung himself around under the platform as Zoya had a few moments before. He grabbed the platform on the other side with his right arm, and used his left to reach for the locket, missing by a hair's breadth.

For a moment, they faced each other silently along the length of the platform.

Then came a cracking sound. The downward jolt of Kane's bulk caused the wood to bend and fracture and a slow fissure started to open across the platform's width. Kane realized what was happening before Zoya, and he tried to make one last leap for safety, but his movement caused the last remaining scraps of wood to crumble away. And he fell.

Zoya lay flat, breathing hard, the locket safe on her chest. With what little energy remained to her, she pulled herself to the edge of the platform and searched the sky for Kane. She found him a few thousand feet below, and watched him grow smaller against the blur of the surface until he was nothing more than a dot.

71

Somehow, Zoya managed to drag herself back onto the *Shadow*. Once she'd recovered enough to stand, she stumbled over to the lever Kane had used to set up the force-field and pulled it down, dropping the blue veil from around the ship. Then she collapsed, exhausted. Vaspine and Rosie were there in an instant, landing a transporter close to where Zoya and Kane had fought. Together, they gathered up Bucker, who was still unconscious, and Zoya, then rushed them back to the *Dragonfly*.

For the next few hours, Vaspine, Rosie, Cid, and a good portion of the crew didn't leave their sides. They were nursed in separate rooms, Zoya in her cabin and Bucker in the captain's quarters, on a makeshift bed. Rosie watched them both and the Doc was there too, trying every medicine they had.

Zoya was the first to wake, opening her eyes a few hours after being picked up. She woke slowly, to the cheers of the crew by her bedside. Vaspine had ordered them to conceal

Bucker's situation from her, so instead they fed her a good meal and called her a hero. Zoya asked them repeatedly where Bucker was. They told her he was recovering.

As it was, another day passed before Bucker came round. The first face he saw was his mother's. They let Zoya in once the Doc was satisfied Bucker was OK. She entered the room quietly, embarrassed about getting him involved in everything, and yet proud of what they'd achieved. She stepped up to his bed and tried to speak, but no words came. What could she say to the boy who'd risked his life to save hers? What could she say to any of them? They'd all done so much. Instead, she leaned in, kissed Bucker on the cheek and whispered, 'Thank you.' She left the room without saying another word.

* * *

Over the following weeks, the ship recovered. Vaspine sent a couple of thieves aboard the *Shadow* to gather up supplies and anything else that might come in useful, then they towed the ship to the skies above a desert and set it on a crash-course. Everybody watched as it sunk to the ground like its captain, exploding in an enormous fireball, the heat of which could be felt thousands of feet up. At the moment of impact, the thieves of the *Dragonfly* cheered.

A couple of days later, an Aviation Army airship making a routine sweep of the skies outside its base happened across a small transporter moving strangely through the sky. The captain of the airship pulled over the transporter and boarded with a team of five men. He found a crowd of sky pirates—half of them the most wanted in the sky—all tied up in a big circle. Before giving them food or water, he asked them to tell him how they had ended up there. They told him all about the *Dragonfly*, about the attack and the brave girl Zoya DeLarose, about the end of the *Shadow* and the death of the most evil sky pirate the world had ever seen.

In time, life on the *Dragonfly* returned to normal. People grew tired of discussing Zoya and Kane and the attack at Dalmacia, and started to talk instead about the weather, or who won at cards, or about the chef's appalling custard. Vaspine ordered the ship to make an extended stop on the Island in the Sky, where it was restocked with enough goods to stay in the air for half a year ('Something tells me we're going to want to keep our heads down for a bit,' said Cid). The captain also had shipbuilders repair the damage done in the ship's fight with Kane, and took a little time to unwind in the cool lakeside air. When they eventually lifted off again, it wasn't to chase after Kane, or anybody, but to go back to doing what they'd always done: rob the rich and give the loot to the people who needed it.

Weeks passed—some good, some bad. With Kane gone, new thieves crept out of the shadows to take his place. None were as villainous as the man in the top hat, but there were enough to ensure the skies remained as dangerous as ever. A rumour emerged of a new threat on the surface, a ragged, pale phantom dressed in shredded black, robbing carts and murdering their owners on lonely country roads. The Aviation Army's surface division investigated, but not a trace of the figure was found, and the rumours were attributed to superstitious farmers and too many mugs of ale.

None of this mattered to Zoya, who spent nearly all of her time with Bucker, causing trouble wherever they could find it. She felt like she was back at the orphanage, a kid again, looked after by the adults, nothing to worry about except what was for dinner. Her wound healed well, and now she had a scar across her ribs to show the other thieves when they were comparing. Bucker recovered too, in time. Rosie declared him even cheekier than before he'd banged his head, but Bucker just denied this and ran off down the ship to find yet more mischief.

When she wasn't with Bucker, Zoya liked to spend her time at the stern of the ship, sitting on a platform similar to the one on which she'd fought Kane. She'd sit there with her dinner on her lap watching the sun sink below the horizon, thinking. Sometimes she'd think of Mr Whycherley, how he'd provided her with a good a start in life, how he'd been so cruelly taken. Other times she'd think of Beebee, a good friend and the bravest man she'd ever met. Mostly, she'd sit there and think of nothing, bouncing up and down on the platform, seeing how high she could go without getting the horrible feeling that she was going to fall. She was happy to be there, happy to be alive, happy to be breathing the fresh air of the sky and eating the good food of the *Dragonfly*.

Vaspine approached her from behind one evening when she was sitting on the platform. 'You're going to fall off one day,' he said.

Zoya chuckled. 'Maybe. It'd be one heck of a fall.' She made space for the captain on the platform. Vaspine sat down, grabbed a sandwich off Zoya's plate and started munching.

'How are you doing?'

'Good,' said Zoya.

'I'm glad,' said Vaspine. 'I've been talking with Rosie and Cid. They told me to come and talk to you.'

'Yeah?'

'It's been six weeks since the *Shadow*,' he continued. 'I wanted to give you a bit of time to rest, recuperate. But I'm aware you don't need to be here any more. Kane's gone. You can go and live a normal life now. No one will bother you. You can go back down to the surface and go back to school and get yourself a normal job.'

'I know,' said Zoya.

'Don't feel like you owe us anything,' continued the captain. 'What we did for you, we'd have done for anyone. Don't feel like you have to pay us back.'

'I don't,' said Zoya.

Vaspine smiled. 'OK,' he said. 'We can drop you off anywhere on the surface. If you don't want to go back to the orphanage, I understand. You've been through a lot. A fresh start's probably a good idea. I know plenty of people who'd take in a girl like you . . .'

'I want to stay,' said Zoya.

'. . . and I'm sure you'd contribute a lot wherever . . .' Vaspine paused. 'Say that again.'

'I want to stay.'

A grin lit up the captain's face. 'I knew it,' he exclaimed. 'I told them. Are you sure?'

'Never been more sure of anything,' said Zoya.

Vaspine put out his hand for Zoya to shake, then tossed it aside when Zoya went for it and grabbed her in a bear hug. 'And we'd love to have you.' He held Zoya at arm's length and regarded her like a proud father. 'You know, you remind me more and more of Jupiter and Dominika every day. They'd be proud of you.'

Zoya smiled. 'They'd be proud of you too, cap'.'

Vaspine smiled back. 'Welcome aboard the *Dragonfly*, DeLarose.'

'Pleasure to be here, captain.'

With that, Vaspine picked up Zoya's plate, pushed himself off the platform and wandered back down the deck towards the mess hall. Zoya sat and thought about what she'd just done. The life of a sky thief—one of intrigue, danger, robbery, under constant threat from the Aviation Army. A part of her felt like she was making a mistake, but a bigger part knew she was doing the right thing. Even at the orphanage she'd felt like an outcast. On the thief ship, skipping through the clouds, hundreds of miles above the earth, with the wind in her hair and a job always there to be done, with everything to learn, friends and good people around her, she realized things had never felt more . . . right. Zoya DeLarose had never felt more at home.

DAN WALKER

Dan Walker, 32, lives smack-bang in the centre of the UK, just outside of a city called Nottingham, with his lovely, patient and supportive partner Dominika.

Dan spent his childhood being dragged up and down the hills of the Peak District, frantically hammering away at computer games and raiding his cousin's bookshelf for anything with a colourful cover. He later tricked the University of Derby into allowing him admission, before graduating with a First Class degree in English. Since then, he has worked with a procession of wonderful people in bookshops, libraries and schools. He currently helps to run a specialist Autism centre.

On the rare occasion you find Dan away from the computer, he can be found trying to tease a melodious sound out of his guitar, re-reading his favourite books for the eighty-eighth time, or fighting off everyone nearby for the last blueberry in the pack.

Zoya's adventures
continue in . . .

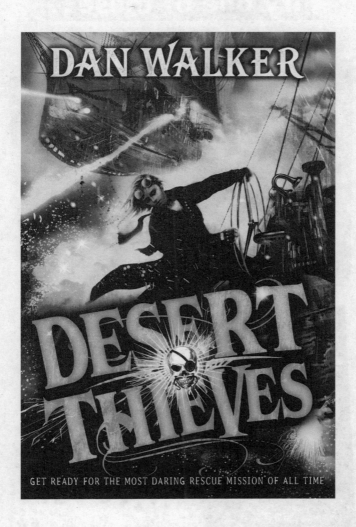

Ready for more great stories?
Try one of these...